CATHY TULLY

Misalignment and Murder

A ChiroCozy Mystery Book 2

First published by Visions and Revisions Unlimited 2021

Copyright © 2021 by Cathy Tully

All rights reserved. No part of this publication may be reproduced, stored or transmitted in any form or by any means, electronic, mechanical, photocopying, recording, scanning, or otherwise without written permission from the publisher. It is illegal to copy this book, post it to a website, or distribute it by any other means without permission.

This novel is entirely a work of fiction. The names, characters and incidents portrayed in it are the work of the author's imagination. Any resemblance to actual persons, living or dead, events or localities is entirely coincidental.

Designations used by companies to distinguish their products are often claimed as trademarks. All brand names and product names used in this book and on its cover are trade names, service marks, trademarks and registered trademarks of their respective owners. The publishers and the book are not associated with any product or vendor mentioned in this book. None of the companies referenced within the book have endorsed the book.

First edition

ISBN: 978-1-7364467-2-0

Cover art by Daniela Colleo of StunningBookCovers.com

This book was professionally typeset on Reedsy.
Find out more at reedsy.com

Contents

Cast of Characters v
Map of Peach Grove, Georgia vii
CHAPTER ONE 1
CHAPTER TWO 6
CHAPTER THREE 11
CHAPTER FOUR 17
CHAPTER FIVE 23
CHAPTER SIX 28
CHAPTER SEVEN 33
CHAPTER EIGHT 37
CHAPTER NINE 41
CHAPTER TEN 46
CHAPTER ELEVEN 50
CHAPTER TWELVE 58
CHAPTER THIRTEEN 61
CHAPTER FOURTEEN 66
CHAPTER FIFTEEN 71
CHAPTER SIXTEEN 74
CHAPTER SEVENTEEN 79
CHAPTER EIGHTEEN 84
CHAPTER NINETEEN 89
CHAPTER TWENTY 93
CHAPTER TWENTY-ONE 97
CHAPTER TWENTY-TWO 103
CHAPTER TWENTY-THREE 108
CHAPTER TWENTY-FOUR 113

CHAPTER TWENTY-FIVE	122
CHAPTER TWENTY-SIX	128
CHAPTER TWENTY-SEVEN	133
CHAPTER TWENTY-EIGHT	139
CHAPTER TWENTY-NINE	143
CHAPTER THIRTY	150
CHAPTER THIRTY-ONE	156
CHAPTER THIRTY-TWO	161
CHAPTER THIRTY-THREE	164
CHAPTER THIRTY-FOUR	170
CHAPTER THIRTY-FIVE	173
CHAPTER THIRTY-SIX	178
CHAPTER THIRTY-SEVEN	183
CHAPTER THIRTY-EIGHT	190
CHAPTER THIRTY-NINE	195
Angie's Italian Frittata	199
Larraine's Three Cheese Macaroni and Cheese.	201
Angie's Pepperoni Lasagna with Marinara sauce	203
Glossary	205
About the Author	206
Also by Cathy Tully	207

Cast of Characters

Susannah's Clan
Larraine Moore - Dr. Shine's Office Manager
Tina Cawthorn - Assistant to Dr. Shine
Angela "Angie" Rossi - Susannah's sister
Caden Rossi - Angie's son
Henry the Eighth - Susannah's Betta fish
Rusty - Office cat

Peach Grove Business Association
Bitsy Long – Owner of Peachy Things
Marcie Jones - Owner of the Wing Shack
Travis Keene - Owner of America's Finest
Maggie Hibbard - Owner of Cutz & Curlz
Daniel Kim - Southside Insurance Agency

Peach Grove Police Department
Randy Laughto - Police Chief
Keith Cawthor - Officer & Tina's husband
Owen Chaffin - Officer
Detective Varina Wither - Detective
Little Junior Long - Desk Sargent

Bitsy's Family
Andrea Long - Bitsy's Niece
Fanny Vincent-Long - Cousin & head cook at Scout camp
Jamal Long - Nephew & Andrea's brother
Kiara Long - Cousin & owner of Apollo

Little Junior Long - Cousin & Sargent at the Peach Grove PD

Shanice Long - Cousin & owner of a print shop

LaDonna Long - Cousin & clerk at the Peach Grove Water Department

Map of Peach Grove, Georgia

CHAPTER ONE

All Hail the Nephew's Here

"Here comes trouble," Dr. Susannah Shine commented to Henry the Eighth, her betta fish, who was swimming circles around the green Marimo moss ball in his tank. Her seven-year-old nephew leapt out of her sister's car and careened toward the front door of Peach Grove Chiropractic. Susannah left her desk to intercept him before he could commence banging.

Caden Rossi ran in, breathless. "Halloween is almost here!" he cried. "Can you take me to the Halloween camp-out this weekend? Jamal and his auntie are going to be there. Can you, can you?" Caden scooped up Rusty, the marmalade cat who called the office his home, and gave him a squeeze.

"Mrow," Rusty said.

Caden ignored him, stroking him with one dirty hand and holding him tight with the other. "I get to sleep in a tent, and cook over a campfire, and go on a haunted trail."

"What's this now?" Susannah turned to her sister, who appeared in the doorway, Caden's backpack and juice box in hand. "Camping? In the woods?"

Angela Rossi ignored the question. "Caden, let go of the cat."

Rusty's golden eyes remained placid as he wiggled until he was dangling by his front paws. He squirmed out of Caden's grasp and sprinted past Angie, who jumped back, grabbing the wall for support. The cat was across the parking lot before she regained her balance. "Only you, Suzie. A bone cracker and a cat rescuer."

Newly relocated from Brooklyn, Angie pronounced the word cracker as *cracka*. Susannah smiled. "We adjust spines, Ange. We don't crack bones."

"Uh-huh." Angie peered down the hall toward the adjusting rooms. "Are ya sure Caden won't bother anyone? I could put off my errands—"

"It's fine." Susannah took Caden's book bag and walked him to the break area, where she placed the book bag on the table. "We have plenty of space away from the patient treatment rooms. Now about this camp-out."

Angie rolled her eyes. "Caden, go wash your hands."

Susannah watched her nephew walk down the hall to the washroom. Asking her newly divorced sister to move in with her had been a spur-of-the-moment decision, and she was shocked and pleased when Angie took her up on it. She and Angie had never been particularly close, and Peach Grove, Georgia, was a far cry from the family home in Brooklyn, New York. After two months, Angie's post-divorce funk was starting to lift, and Caden seemed to be thriving. He had confided in her that he didn't want to go to the Fall Festival, but Angie made no mention of that. Being an aunt was sometimes more than Susannah had bargained for. "You know I hate being in the woods."

"Yeah, about that. Ya know I wouldn't ask if I didn't have to." Angie shook out her black hair and gazed up at her younger sister. Her Brooklyn accent caused her to pronounce ask as *axe*. Susannah shuddered. She had lived in small-town Georgia for a long time—so long that a soft country accent sounded more familiar than Angie's New York City Yankee twang. "The hospital scheduled a CPR and Advanced Life Support training for Saturday morning, and I hafta attend."

Susannah chewed her lip. She'd been thrilled when Angie found a position at Henry County Hospital. She was a little less thrilled now. As for the camp-out, after an unpleasant incident over the summer, her appreciation for the outdoor life had waned. Fearing an Italian-American intervention featuring her mother's Rosary Society, she had kept the details of the unpleasantness from her family in New York, and she wasn't going to mention them to Angie now.

Angie squinted at her, a trait Susannah knew meant she was ready to argue. "Bitsy is taking Jamal. Maybe you can share a tent. Keith will be there too. You have nothing to worry about."

"I'm not worried. I—" Susannah stopped. Caden appeared in the hallway, and Angie rushed to him; she planted a loud kiss on the top of his head and led him back down the hall to the break area. Susannah noted a fleeting expression of doubt sweep across Angie's features and then disappear. It was her turn to reassure her sister. "He's going to be fine."

Angie nodded at Susannah and pulled a lipstick from her purse. She looked around. Susannah knew Angie was searching for a mirror. Foundation, eyeliner, and blush were what Angie called her first line of defense. Mascara, eye shadow, and a custom lipstick color, which Angie called Marvelous Magenta, finished the tableau. Susannah would have looked like a clown with that much makeup on, but set off by Angie's olive skin and black hair, it looked amazing. "Don't forget, the Fall Festival is tonight at school." She dropped the lipstick into her bag and pointed down the hall to the break area. "I already stocked the fridge so yas can have a hot meal before ya go. I know me leaving early for my shift is throwing a monkey wrench into your schedule, but once I'm done with training, I won't need you to watch him as much." Like most in her family, Angie was a lover of Italian food. But Angie was also a tireless cook, using all the family recipes and updating and inventing her own gourmet takes on them. She laughed at Susannah's simple way of eating and food sensitivities. "Go to work."

Twenty minutes later, Susannah entered treatment room two where Gus Arnold, the assistant principal at Peach Grove Elementary School, sat. His blond hair and deep-set gray-blue eyes gave him a Ryan Gosling look, only blonder.

"Dr. Shine." He smiled at her. "That last adjustment fixed my knee pain. I've felt better in the last month than I have in the last year. And I've gotten off all my pain medications."

"I'm glad to hear it." Susannah held up her hand for a high five.

"Me too." He laughed as he high-fived her. "But yesterday, I was walking around my yard and stepped in a hole, and I think I misaligned my knee. The pain is back. I need another adjustment."

"I can arrange that." Susannah faced Gus and positioned his leg for the adjustment, wrapping her hands around his knee while he lay on his back. A low, deep click signaled a successful adjustment.

Gus sat up, tentatively putting his weight on his leg. "I can't believe the difference. I wish I had done this years ago."

"That's what they all say."

CHAPTER ONE

Gus took a few steps, placing more and more weight on the joint. "Thank goodness, the pain is gone. You have no idea how much this helps me. Tonight's the Fall Festival at school. I've been on my feet constantly the last few days."

Susannah took a moment to ask Gus about what to expect at a Fall Festival, and he filled her in. His gracious manner and infectious smile put her at ease.

"I'll see you there." He did a herky-jerky step and laughed as he left the room.

Peach Grove was in autumn mode, and this year she would have the added enjoyment of accompanying Caden to the festival. As she watched Gus leave the treatment room, another thought came to her: in addition to the Fall Festival tonight and the camp-out this weekend, tomorrow morning another local institution was meeting. The Peach Grove Business Association would elect a new president, and her best friend, Bitsy Long, was running. Whatever the outcome, this was going to be an interesting week.

CHAPTER TWO

A Zombie in the Sand

Susannah entered her office and was startled to see Caden with his cheek pressed against the glass of Henry the Eighth's fish tank. Henry swam his usual route as Caden watched, wide-eyed, his small body slumped sideways in a chair, one finger tracking the fish as he swished by. The glass on the tank fogged from Caden's breath.

Susannah said, "You never told me why you don't want to go to the Fall Festival."

Caden blew on the tank and ran his finger through the condensation. "Some of the kids are mean to me. Dylan S. laughs at me. He says I talk funny."

Susannah felt her stomach sink. His New York accent was not as pronounced as Angie's, but it was clear he wasn't from around here. She put her hand on his shoulder. "Don't pay attention to Dylan S., he sounds like a real doofus."

Caden sat up and smiled. "Yeah, he's a doo-puss."

"Not doo-puss, doofus. It means he's dumb."

"Oh. I think he's a doo-puss too."

Susannah shook her head, not sure if she had just made the matter worse. "Come on, let's go have some fun." She grabbed

CHAPTER TWO

his backpack and loaded him into her Jeep.

Her last patient had been running late, and they were behind. Luckily, Peach Grove Elementary was only minutes from the office. When they arrived, a Peach Grove Police Department patrol car blocked the entrance to the parking lot. Officer Owen Chaffin, who Susannah had met over the weekend at Tina and Keith Cawthorn's Halloween party, waved her toward the other cars parked behind the school.

Caden pressed his nose to the window. "Are we really allowed to park on the lawn?"

Susannah chuckled. The overflow parking was in the grassy field past the playground. In Brooklyn, where Caden came from, the only wide-open green spaces were parks surrounded by cement walkways and chain link fences. In fact, some of the parks in Brooklyn *were* just cement walkways and chain link fences. "Only tonight, kid. Too many cars to fit in the lot."

The Jeep bumped over the rutted grass, and she squeezed into the last spot next to some cedar trees. She led Caden across the playground, toward the gymnasium, passing Bitsy's SUV on the way. The air smelled of hay and freshly popped popcorn. Bales were stacked two and three high, with gap-toothed jack-o'-lanterns and scarecrows lounging on top. Strains of "Turkey in the Straw" filled the air, and children and adults lined up to play games along a midway. At the far end of the building were a dunking booth and a bouncy house.

She looked around for Bitsy, who would be accompanying Jamal, but didn't see her. Caden found his classmates and queued up to try his hand at knocking down a pyramid of empty soda cans with a tennis ball. As he took his turn, a loud whoop caught Susannah's attention, and she proceeded down the midway. When she saw the source of the whoop, she laughed out loud and called Caden over.

Bitsy stood in the dunking tank, water cascading off her body. She was dressed as a scarecrow, her straw hat drooping. Jamal stood in front of the booth, and Caden ran to his side.

"That's Jamal's auntie," he giggled. "She looks funny. She's got straw in her hair."

Susannah watched as Bitsy's colorful costume and lively banter kept the adults around the dunk tank. A few moms cheered delightedly when she splashed down. Each time a bull's-eye pitched Bitsy off her perch, Caden and Jamal capered to and fro in front of the tank, like oversized puppies, soaking up almost as much moisture as she did. After an hour, Bitsy had raised $300 for the PTA and was as wrinkly as a box of raisins. She exited the booth with a lopsided smile and a wilted straw hat. She was immediately set upon by the boys, who, if they'd had a dry spot on them, immediately lost it. Susannah kept her distance as Bitsy rained on the pavement.

"That dunking tank is hungry work." Bitsy hugged Jamal and winked at Caden. "What do you say we go get ourselves some kettle corn?"

The boys nodded enthusiastically.

"Can I, Aunt Suzie?" asked Caden.

"Sure, you stick with Ms. Bitsy while I get you some dry clothes out of the car."

Susannah hurried away, crossing the playground quickly. The streetlight from the parking lot shone an orange haze across the swing set and sandbox. Digging in her purse for her keys as she went, she stopped. Had she heard a noise? She looked around, but all she saw was a teacher cleaning up her game station in the parking lot. Glancing at the row of cedar trees, she reached her Jeep and jumped in. As she pulled the door shut, "Girl on Fire," the ringtone she had assigned to Bitsy, sounded from her purse.

"Kettle corn's almost all gone," Bitsy crowed. "What's taking you so long?"

Susannah wedged the phone between her shoulder and ear as she twisted to reach the back seat. "I'm coming. Save me some," she replied, grabbing the gym bag jammed with emergency supplies.

"You snooze, you lose," Bitsy replied. The call ended and Susannah tossed the phone into her bag, shaking her head with a smile. As she pulled out a pair of blue jeans and a T-shirt from the gym bag, she had the feeling that she was being watched and again gazed down the row of cedar trees. Not a soul graced either the paved lot or the grassy overflow parking.

Suddenly a scream split the quiet. Her heart began hammering so strongly, she could hear her pulse in her ears. She shouldered her bag and grabbed her keys. The slam of the door fell flat in the still night air. Hustling across the parking lot, she passed the sandbox and swings. A loud groan sent the hair on her arms standing straight up. She turned and saw someone dressed as a zombie coming from the trees. Trembling, she forced a smile. *Probably some middle schooler trying to scare me.*

"Dr. Shine."

The zombie had called her name. She stopped, watching the costumed teen shamble toward her, one leg dragging behind in a classic zombie cadence. Suddenly the zombie tripped and fell face down into the sandbox. Susannah clutched her keys, her hand shaking. Again the zombie called her name and she drew closer, horrified to see a dark substance seep into the sand beneath its hips.

That's blood!

She rushed over. "Ack!" she blurted. This was not a teen. It was a man, face down, sprawled with one arm pinned underneath his body. She turned him over and gasped.

"Gus!"

Blood seeped from a hole in his chest.

CHAPTER THREE

Cedar Later

Bitsy Long leaned over the hood of her SUV, a pair of binoculars in her hand. She appeared to be scanning the cedar trees that separated the school grounds from the library next door. Susannah glanced toward the police cars and crime scene tape. The police techs had descended on the playground while uniformed officers, including Officer Chaffin, who had been first on the scene, walked the tree line, probably looking for evidence. Chief Randy Laughton leaned against his patrol car. Next to him, Detective Varina Withers folded her arms and glared at Susannah. The detective had agreed to take her statement after Caden left with Jamal and was now waiting impatiently for her. Susannah tapped lightly on Bitsy's shoulder.

"Sweet sugar!" Bitsy jumped and turned on Susannah, brandishing the binoculars with a shaking hand. "Don't scare me like that when I'm scanning for zombies."

Susannah bit her lip. "There are no zombies."

"Don't fib to me, I know that Mr. Gus was zombie-ized." She shot a glance at Randy. "Even though the police deny it."

"I'm not fibbing. He was just wearing Halloween makeup."

"Hummph." She leaned in and whispered, "Do you double-pinky-swear?"

Susannah suppressed an eye roll. She leaned in and offered up her pinky, which Bitsy grabbed with her orange-lacquered little finger.

"Now, get out of here before you scare the boys."

Susannah glanced into the back seat. Jamal had his slender arm around Caden's shoulder as they munched popcorn and stared at Bitsy's phone. Susannah felt her stomach drop. So far she was a horrible failure at being an aunt. Less than an hour into her first full foray into aunt-hood, she had to abandon her nephew. Well, maybe not abandon. After all, Bitsy was an adult. Susannah said, "You'd better take them to your house. The kettle corn is going to run out soon, and then they'll want to know what's going on."

Bitsy eyed the half-empty bag of kettle corn that lay across the boys' legs. Her eyes lit up, emphasizing the smattering of freckles across her nose and cheeks. "I am getting a little peckish myself. That bag might not last much longer."

Susannah held the door and nudged Bitsy into the driver's seat. Despite the chill growing in the October air, she was beginning to sweat. "I'll call you when I get home."

Bitsy replied with a thumbs-up and left.

Susannah strode toward the police chief's car, glancing at her Jeep, which now looked forlorn in the dark. A slight breeze blew, causing her skin to break into gooseflesh, yet the twenty-foot-tall cedar trees barely moved. Little wonder she hadn't seen anything earlier in the evening. The lower boughs were so large, it would take gale-force winds to move them. Gus could have been behind them the whole time, and she never would have known.

CHAPTER THREE

The radio crackled to life, and Chief Laughton slid into his vehicle. Officer Chaffin, his canvas of the crime scene over, walked toward her. "Dr. Shine," he began, his voice a tone lower than she remembered it. Then again, she had only met him briefly at Tina's Halloween party. Could she actually recall what he sounded like? "Is there anything more you remember?" he asked.

Susannah shook her head. He had questioned her initially, but there was nothing more she could say. He looked worried, and Susannah didn't blame him. A murder had been committed right under his nose. She was sure Detective Withers, who was giving the young officer a hard stare, would have something to say about it.

The detective came over and raised her eyebrow at the officer, who walked away. "Officer Chaffin tells me that that you found Mr. Arnold's body." The statement came out like an accusation.

"Actually, he found me."

Detective Withers pulled a small notepad out of her pocket. "Explain."

"I was walking to the school from my car, and I heard a noise. I didn't see him at first. He must have come out of the trees." Susannah gazed at the sandbox. What an undignified place to die.

The detective made a note. "What kind of noise did you hear?"

"Uh, I'm not sure. I was scrounging in my purse for my keys. And then I heard a scream. I didn't hear a gunshot. I thought it was some kids horsing around." Susannah didn't want to admit that the noise had spooked her. "So at first I didn't stop and look at him carefully. I thought it was a Halloween prank."

The detective motioned to Susannah's Jeep with her pen. "Why did you park all the way over there?"

"I was running late, and it was the last spot open."

The detective, her eyes narrowing, wrote some more. When Susannah had first met her, she had thought that the detective's eyes had a serpentine appearance, but she didn't see that anymore. The detective looked up from her pad.

"We'll be in touch." The detective flipped her notepad closed and went to confer with Chief Laughton. After a few minutes, the detective returned. "I'll contact you to take a formal statement."

Susannah, preoccupied, drove the short way to Bitsy's house. She retrieved Caden but politely declined Bitsy's invitation to stay for dinner. As she returned home, she replayed the details in her mind. She had heard a noise and thought it came from the school. But it must have been Gus. She shivered as the Jeep jostled its way over the railroad tracks and Caden giggled. Turning her attention to him, she pushed her most recent brush with death to the back of her mind. An hour later, as Caden soaked in the tub, Susannah leaned her elbows on her kitchen counter and sighed. The pink-and-white demitasse cup she held had been given to her by her Nana and reminded her of home. She inhaled deeply. The aroma of espresso filled her senses and enlivened her brain. She drank the shot in one gulp. Pulling her phone from her pocket, she flopped down on the couch to send Angie a text. As Caden sang in the tub, she tapped a message, stopped, read what she'd written and erased it. She repeated the sequence twice more, and finally settled on: *Call me, important.*

As she was tucking Caden into bed, her phone rang. After listening to Caden tell his mother good night, Susannah took

CHAPTER THREE

the phone into the other room and broke the news to Angie. She was surprised when she heard her sister sobbing. "Ange, are you okay?"

"I can't believe it. I just saw him. How can he be dead?"

Susannah was at a loss for words. Did Angie always get so attached to Caden's teachers so quickly? If Gus had not been a patient, she probably wouldn't have even remembered his name.

"I gotta find a Kleenex," Angie continued, snuffling. She honked into the phone. "Who would want to kill him? He was a grammar school principal."

"I dunno," Susannah mumbled. "The principal is your pal."

"*Madonna mia!*" Angie yelled. "Are you insane, joking at a time like this?"

"No, I just meant—"

"I must have been crazy to move here. I lived my whole life in Brooklyn, the crime capital of the Western world, and no one's grammar school principal ever got shot. How am I gonna tell Ma?"

Susannah blanched at the thought that her family in Brooklyn would find out about this.

"I gotta go, Suzie." Angie was whispering now. "We'll talk about this later."

Susannah stared at the screen as it toned and went silent. She put the phone on vibrate and tossed it on the couch. Not the reaction she'd been expecting. She hadn't realized that Angie had seen Gus when she picked up Caden from school. As Susannah gripped the TV remote, a muted buzz sounded from the cushion next to her. Probably Angie, calling to apologize.

Susannah reached for the phone, surprised to see the image of Bitsy. Though she just wanted to sink into the couch hugging a pillow, she took the call. She understood Bitsy's need to dissect the events of the day, especially in light of the fact that Bitsy was now guardian to her nephew. They spoke for several minutes, Susannah changing the subject to tomorrow's Business Association meeting as soon as she could. Bitsy filled Susannah in on her newest strategies for her presidential bid. At least the election in the morning was something to look forward to. When the call was done, Susannah sighed and turned on the TV, settling in to wait for Angie.

She woke in the middle of the night with a kink in her neck. She glanced at the clock: 2:15 a.m. Why hadn't Angie awakened her? Susannah picked herself up and tumbled onto her bed without even undressing.

CHAPTER FOUR

Growl-A-Ween

After dropping Caden off at school, Susannah pulled up outside Bitsy's Queen Anne Victorian, which was decked out for Halloween. Strings of purple and orange fairy lights hung from the posts and wrapped around the rails of her porch. Bitsy sat on the edge of a red wooden swing that was a refreshing counterpoint to the white porch and railings. When she saw Susannah, she bolted off the swing and shot down the steps, a biscuit in hand. The swing pitched behind her.

"Thanks for carrying me to the meeting," she said as she opened the Jeep's door and hopped into the passenger seat. "What with all these zombies on the loose, I'd rather travel in pairs."

"No problem." Susannah bit her lip. Sometimes it was better to ignore Bitsy's comments than to have to decide whether or not she was kidding. "I wouldn't miss this vote for the world."

Bitsy popped the remainder of the biscuit in her mouth as Susannah put the Jeep in gear. "Nervous?" asked Susannah.

"Excited is more like it," Bitsy replied, chewing thoughtfully. "When I'm president, there's gonna be big changes."

"Like what?"

"Like, I'm gonna shake the straw out of the Peach Grove Business Association." Bitsy stared out the window as they crossed the railroad tracks and sailed through downtown Peach Grove. She pointed to the green space across from her shop, Peachy Things, where a mass of scarecrows congregated. Every year, the PGBA invited local businesses to each build a scarecrow and place it on the city green. It gave an autumn flavor to the downtown shopping area. Bitsy had always enjoyed dressing her scarecrow. "See that, that's the old PGBA. I'm gonna ring in the new PGBA."

"How?"

"Oh, you'll see." Bitsy pointed at her with a long fingernail. "I don't want to muddy my vision by putting it out into the world prematurely."

They drove the rest of the way in silence. The meeting was held at the takeout restaurant of the outgoing president, Marcie Jones. Susannah found the last parking place in the strip of stores that included the Wing Shack. Exiting the Jeep, she pointed to a pickup truck with a rifle rack. "Whose truck is that?"

"Travis Keene, owner of America's Finest Sporting Goods. He and Maggie have been dating a while now." Bitsy opened the Wing Shack's door, smiling at Maggie Hibbard, a new member whose beauty shop, Cutz & Curlz, had been open less than a year. "Hey, Miss Maggie, I see you finally got Travis to join."

Marcie rushed over, frowning at the scuff marks Travis's cowboy boots made on the floor. "We just opened the meeting. First order of business is the vote. Daniel just addressed the group." Daniel Kim, owner of the Southside Insurance Agency, was Bitsy's opponent. Marcie handed Susannah a slip of paper

CHAPTER FOUR

and turned to Bitsy. "You can say a few words if you'd like."

Bitsy sauntered over to the counter. The Wing Shack was a takeout joint with a few small tables scattered throughout a tiled dining area. Today's meeting had every chair filled. Bitsy waved at the room with the slip of paper flapping between her fingers. "Y'all know me. I've been runnin' Peachy Things for over fifteen years. If you elect me, I'll keep things going just like Marcie has, with maybe a little peachy pizazz." She waved the ballot. "Let's vote so we can go eat."

There was a murmur of approval and rustle of paper. When all the votes were collected, Marcie hooked Susannah's arm, "Dr. Shine is going to witness the counting of the ballots." With that, Marcie pulled her into the kitchen and threw the ballots on the long stainless steel counter.

Susannah gazed around the room at the refrigerated cases and walk-in freezer. For years the PGBA had met at Anita Alvarez's restaurant, the Cantina Caliente. That had all changed over the summer when Anita was murdered. Since then Marcie had taken on the duty of hosting the meetings, and not every memory Susannah had of this kitchen was pleasant. She turned her attention to Marcie, who had recently resigned as president—everyone assumed because of the turmoil caused by her husband, Billy. She had agreed to stay on to oversee the election, but when it was done, she would be gone. The competition for her position had been less than cutthroat, but Daniel had put up a valiant fight against Bitsy. Susannah peered at Marcie's notepad. It looked like Bitsy was out in front.

Susannah smiled. Bitsy had a casual, even flaky style, but she was grounded in solid business practices, which she had learned not from her stint at the Savannah College of Art and Design but through her large family, who had several business owners among them. Uncle Jesse Long, who owned a construction company, was primary among Bitsy's mentors. Susannah had a fondness for him, as he had helped her out of a jam when she was building her chiropractic office.

Marcie pushed a pile of folded rectangles of paper across the counter to Susannah. "Will you verify my count, please?"

Glancing at the hash marks Marcie had scratched on her notepad, Susannah reached for the pile of paper. She went through the ballots and then wrote her tallies under Marcie's and initialed them. Marcie peered at Susannah, who suddenly realized that Marcie's eyes were bloodshot and glassy. Was she going to cry? Before Susannah could say anything, Marcie said, "I wanted to let you know that I'm closing the Wing Shack and moving."

Susannah gasped, "But why?"

Marcie gave her a wan smile. "You know why." She sighed. "I can't keep coming here every day, it's too painful. I want to be closer to Hayle. With her school schedule, she rarely visits."

"Oh," Susannah managed.

"I want you to know that I don't blame you."

Open-mouthed, Susannah stared at Marcie, who held up a finger and shook her head slightly, as if to say: *Don't say anything.* "Well then." Marcie glanced into the dining room. "Let's go."

The women entered the dining room and Marcie faced the members.

"Before I announce the winner, I want to remind you that we still need volunteers for our annual Halloween event." Marcie picked a clipboard up off the takeout counter and handed it to Susannah. With a tilt of her head, she effectively telegraphed the words *what are you waiting for, pass this around.* Susannah

CHAPTER FOUR

took the pen Marcie was pushing into her hand, scratched her name on the first line of the list, and handed it off to Maggie Hibbard, who signed her name and passed it on.

Maggie smiled and whispered to Susannah, "Is your nephew excited about the Halloween camp-out? My boys are over the moon." She tilted her head at Travis Keene. "It's our first camp-out as a couple. Though he'll be with the leaders and I'll be with the boys."

"Caden can't wait. I'll be taking him. My sister has to work."

"Wonderful—"

Marcie cleared her throat. "We will again be sponsoring the Trunk-or-Treat festivities at the Peach Grove Municipal Building." Marcie continued, "And I'm sure our new president, Bitsy Long, will do us proud."

There was a murmur of approval with light applause as Bitsy sashayed to the counter. Marcie slipped away and disappeared into the kitchen. Bitsy held up her hands. "Thank you to all who voted for me. And to all who didn't…" She stuck her tongue out at Daniel Kim and then chortled. He grinned and waved back. "But seriously, I consider myself lucky to have this job."

Someone from the group called out, "No speech, let's eat."

Bitsy waved at the group. "A man after my own heart." After the laughter died down, Bitsy continued. "Just one order of business. I already ran this by the mayor, and she is on board one hundred percent."

The room went quiet, and Marcie reappeared from the depths of the kitchen and stood next to the iced tea urn, a puzzled look on her face.

"Ladies and gentlemen of the Peach Grove Business Association, we are the proud sponsors of Growl-A-Ween, our first annual canine costume contest."

CHAPTER FIVE

Ladies' Crime-Solving Club

Susannah entered through the rear door of Peach Grove Chiropractic and threw her purse on the table in the break area. Over the summer, when she had been under suspicion of murdering Anita Alvarez, this break area had hosted several meetings of her closest friends. Dubbed the Ladies' Crime-Solving Club by Bitsy, today their early get together would be a celebration of Bitsy's victory.

As she closed the door, Susannah watched Larraine Moore, her office manager, pull into the parking lot. Larraine exited her Mercury Grand Marquis, made her way to the passenger door, and helped Tina Cawthorn, now six months pregnant, out of the passenger seat. Tina handed Larraine a plate, wrapped in plastic wrap, and a four-pack of Starbucks coffee. The plate looked like it was piled high with homemade cookies. Larraine was on the welcoming committee at the Peach Grove Baptist Church and was always ready to ply newcomers with baked goods. Larraine entered first, with Rusty hot on her heels and making a figure eight around her legs.

Larraine's smile faded. "Where's Bitsy?"

"She's—" A loud thud interrupted Susannah, and she sped

down the main hall, calling over her shoulder, "At the front door." Another thump resounded in the morning air, and Susannah snapped open the deadbolt and threw the door wide. Bitsy came in.

"It's about time." Bitsy stood with one hand on her hip.

"Excuse me, Your Worshipfulness." Susannah rolled her eyes. "You could have parked in the back like everyone else."

"And risk a supernatural incident? I think not. I'll stick to your ghost-free lot, thank you."

"Here she is," Larraine called when Bitsy approached. "Madam President."

Bitsy bowed as she entered the break room, and Larraine embraced her, adding a pat on the back. Tina emerged from the kitchen with a handful of napkins. "Congratulations."

"Thank you." Bitsy bowed low, one leg behind her.

Susannah smiled, remembering that Bitsy had once mentioned a dream of being on the stage. She laughed. A loud *meow* and a nudge against her leg turned her attention to Rusty. As the women settled in with their coffee, she filled Rusty's bowl with kibble. Rusty looked up at her, golden eyes unblinking, and she gave him a few strokes before shutting the door and taking a seat.

"Every celebration needs a treat." Larraine pointed to the plate on the table. "Lucky I had a plate of Miss Shirleen's pumpkin chocolate chip cookies, so enjoy."

"There's fruit and yogurt in the kitchen," Susannah told Tina, who smiled but looked elsewhere. Susannah, who followed a gluten- and allergen-free diet, always kept the fridge stocked with healthy snacks.

"I already had a good breakfast." Tina reached for a small cookie. "So I'm only going to have a taste."

CHAPTER FIVE

The women held their paper cups high and toasted Bitsy's good news.

"By the way, I've got some info about Gus," Tina said, placing the uneaten part of her cookie on a napkin. All eyes were on her. Tina's husband, Keith Cawthorn, was a Peach Grove police officer, and she often gleaned information from him. "I overheard Keith say that Gus's car was found in the library parking lot. The police think he was meeting someone." She put the words *meeting someone* in air quotes.

The room went silent. Over the summer, there had been much discussion among the women about whether Anita Alvarez had been "meeting someone" for a romantic rendezvous when she was killed. The women looked at each other knowingly.

"Little Junior tells me the same," Bitsy said, popping half a cookie into her mouth and washing it down with a gulp of Starbucks. Little Junior Long, the desk sergeant at the Peach Grove PD, was one of Bitsy's many cousins. Susannah often wondered if he could read lips because no detail ever seemed to escape his grasp. "But there's more. They definitely think he was meeting a woman. She left something in his car, but Little Junior wasn't sure what it was."

The women looked at each other. Could a woman have killed Gus?

"Anything else from Little Junior?" Susannah asked.

"No." Bitsy shook her head as she drank. "Just that it was something small."

"That sounds like an important clue," Larraine said.

"It could be," Susannah said. "But it doesn't really involve us."

The room was silent except for Bitsy slurping her coffee.

Larraine and Tina exchanged a glance, and Tina turned to gape at Susannah, the gold flecks in her brown eyes shining.

"What?" Susannah asked.

"Not involve us?" Tina looked incredulous. "Dr. Shine, you found Gus's body. You remember what happened the last time you discovered a recently deceased acquaintance?"

"Well, yes, but—"

"No buts," Larraine said, peering over her bifocals at Susannah. "We need to be proactive here. We can't wait until that detective accuses you. Again. We should start now."

"I agree," Bitsy added. "There's something not right about this whole thing. I know where to start. At the fall festival, I made some new friends who are on the PTA."

Tina poked Larraine's arm. "We heard you made a big splash there," Larraine said, chuckling. Tina laughed. They clearly had both heard about Bitsy's stint in the dunking booth.

"I suppose I did," Bitsy said, smiling.

"Okay," Susannah agreed, then sipped coffee off the plastic lid of her Starbucks cup. "I guess I'll follow up with Angie. Maybe she's heard something that would be helpful." Susannah glanced at her phone, then pointed at Larraine and Tina. "It's ten am. Patients aren't due in until three o'clock. Bitsy will make contact with the PTA. I'm going to go home and check on Angie, and I'll see you two around noon."

Tina and Larraine nodded their agreement. Susannah glanced at the women. Though glad that Angie had joined her in Georgia, these women had sustained her when her family was far away. Bitsy and the Long clan had welcomed Susannah into their fold over fifteen years ago, and she loved every minute of time she spent with them. Larraine had been her office manager for almost as long, and Susannah congratulated herself on a regular basis for being smart enough to hire the woman. Tina, though younger, had fallen into the rhythm of the office and become part of the furniture, so to speak. She considered all of them family. Together, the four of them would make sense of Gus's death.

CHAPTER SIX

Cookin' N Cryin'

Susannah entered her house on tiptoe. Angie's car was parked in the driveway, and Susannah expected to find her sister in bed with the blanket pulled over her head. But when she pushed the door open, she was greeted by the smell of something burning and the sound of the TV blaring. Rushing into the kitchen, Susannah switched the flame off and moved a saucepan to another burner. Inside the pot, shrunken bits of garlic were black and smoldering.

"Angie?" Susannah called. There was no answer. In the living room, Angie slumped on the couch watching *The Price Is Right*, a tissue in her hand. "Angie." Susannah picked up the remote and muted Drew Carey. "What's going on? What are you cooking?"

Angie jumped up from the couch. "My sauce!" she cried in a congested nasal tone as she ran into the kitchen. Grabbing a dishtowel, she began waving it around to dissipate the smoke. "The garlic is burning."

"The garlic is burnt," Susannah replied. "Why are you cooking? You should be in bed. What time did you get in last night?"

"I can't sleep. I thought I'd start a lasagna." Angie's lasagna with meat sauce was famous in their family. She used the old family recipe, tweaking it with a bit of pepperoni to make the whole dish a spice-filled cheesy delight. Susannah's mouth watered at the thought. Angie peered into the saucepan, her shoulders drooping. Her ratty bathrobe hung off her frame. Even her black curls seemed to lack their usual bounce.

Susannah grabbed two potholders, lifted the pot from the stove, and poured the burnt oil and garlic into the trash can. "I'll clean it up." Susannah placed the pot in the sink with a sizzle of water against hot stainless steel.

Angie looked at her feet. "Okay." Her nasal congestion made the word sound like *otay*. Susannah gave her a hug. Angie huffed a few times against Susannah's chest, then stepped back. Uncurling her fist, she wiped her nose with a crumpled tissue. A flicker of anger showed in her black eyes. "I hate crying!"

Susannah patted her back. "It's going to be all right."

"I hate crying." Angie blew her nose into the used tissue. "My nose gets red." *Nose* sounded like *dose*.

"I know." Susannah chuckled and then inhaled sharply. She didn't want to insult her again by laughing.

Angie gave Susannah a squeeze. "I'm sorry, Suzie."

"For what?"

"For bitin' your head off last night. I was just so surprised about Gus's death. I mean, I never expected to hear this kind of news. Just when things seemed to be going my way."

"Things still are going your way. You have a good job. You have some great friends. Caden is making friends too, except for Dylan S., who we both agree is a doofus."

Angie smiled. "The problem isn't Caden," Angie grabbed Susannah's shirt and pulled her closer; her eyes were steely.

Susannah felt a chill go down her arms. Angie lowered her voice. "It's me."

"I—"

"It's me. I mess things up everywhere I go."

"Don't say that, Angie. None of this is your fault."

"You don't understand." Angie closed her eyes and leaned her head back. Her eyelashes were tinged with smudges of mascara that hadn't been removed properly. Her lips looked naked with no lipstick. Susannah wanted to reassure Angie, but the wild look on her sister's face stopped her. Angie opened her eyes and said, "You know what I need?"

"No," Susannah said cautiously. "What do you need?"

"I need to clean this up and start again." She ripped a paper towel from the roll. At the sink, she wiped out the inside of the saucepan and threw the paper towel in the trash. Running the water at full force, she scrubbed the saucepan, setting up for another batch. "This sauce has to simmer for at least six hours."

Susannah watched her sister. She knew people dealt with stress in different ways. Some people cleaned, others ate, or smoked. Angie cooked. But why was she taking this so hard? "Why don't you get some sleep? I can pick Caden up from school later and after I'm through with patients, I'll take us all out to dinner."

"Nah, I already have all the ingredients."

Susannah opened her refrigerator. Seeing it packed to the brim with food still surprised her. An extra-large container of ricotta cheese took up part of the top shelf. A block of mozzarella cheese and a stick of pepperoni were in there somewhere. She shot a glance at Angie, who had stopped crying and was humming to herself. Grabbing a bottle of iced tea, she closed the door. "All right, then. But I insist on picking up Caden after school. By the time you're done cooking, you'll be exhausted. He can hang with me at the office while you catch a nap."

Angie nodded. "You're probably right. Thanks."

* * *

Susannah reached out and steadied the top-of-the-line air mattress, which teetered precariously across the length of Bitsy's shopping cart. A tent, sleeping bags, and Merrell hiking shoes filled the basket. After Susannah's chiropractic patients had gone, Bitsy appeared, convincing Susannah to come shopping for gear for the camp-out. Caden had been more than happy to spend time with Jamal and his big sister Andrea, so a bargain had been struck.

Finally satisfied, Bitsy pushed her buggy toward the checkout area of America's Finest Sporting Goods, where they found Travis Keene at the register.

"Gettin' ready for the Halloween camping trip?" Travis sponsored Caden and Jamal's Cub Scout troop and also helped Keith out with the meetings. The troop parents returned the favor by patronizing his store in lieu of the big box sporting goods store up the road. Bitsy's shopping cart was a testament to that. Travis scratched his beard with the back of his fingers.

"We sure are," Bitsy said, piling the belt with her goods. "Jamal is so excited, he can't talk about anything else."

"Youngin's are adorable." He touched a cigarette tucked behind his ear. "Mine're excited about it too. But right now we're talkin' 'bout something else." Travis spoke of Maggie's two sons as if they were his own.

Bitsy leaned forward as she loaded her hiking boots onto the conveyor belt. There wasn't much in the county that got by the Long clan. Travis's statement was like a challenge to Bitsy's whole family. "Like what?"

"Like a nine-millimeter gun killed Gus Arnold."

"Where'd you hear that?" Bitsy asked.

"I reckon I have my sources." Travis scanned the tent and sleeping bags and totaled Bitsy's order. Like a sleight-of-hand trick, the cigarette went from behind his ear and into his mouth. "Most of the Peach Grove PD comes here for one thing or t'other."

Bitsy nodded but said nothing. Had Little Junior missed a key bit of information?

Susannah's phone rang, and she stepped away to answer it. She frowned at the unknown number and then accepted the call.

Angie's voice came through. "Suzie? Can you come and get me? I'm in jail."

CHAPTER SEVEN

Angie's Key

Susannah peered down the hood of her Jeep, staring at the road as if silently willing the pavement to turn into the parking lot of the police station. The drive was only two minutes from the sporting goods store, but her arrival had been delayed by Bitsy insisting that she ride along with Susannah. Sitting in the passenger seat, Bitsy tapped on her phone, her long nails clacking against the screen, and said, "I don't understand why Little Junior didn't text me."

Susannah said nothing as she replayed the events of the last day and didn't like what she saw. Angie's reaction to Gus's death had seemed odd, but her sister was prone to bursting into sobs over a bad haircut. But there was more to it than that. What exactly did she mean by *I mess things up everywhere I go*?

She was roused from her thoughts by Bitsy slapping her phone onto her thigh. "He's at the dentist!" she declared.

Susannah pulled into the Peach Grove PD parking lot, a place that was familiar for all the wrong reasons. She bit her lip. "Who's at the dentist?"

"Little Junior." Bitsy picked up her phone and sliced the air with it as she spoke. "He got a bad toothache yesterday and had to make an emergency appointment with his dentist. That's why I didn't know none of this was coming. I'm sorry."

Little Junior couldn't be everywhere. "Not his fault." The memory of Angie's late arrival home the night Gus was killed sent chills down Susannah's arms. Had she come home at all that night? Yes—Caden had said she was there in the morning and then left. What was she doing? "Stay here," Susannah told Bitsy.

"Oh, no. You need a calm-headed presence with you."

Butterflies in her stomach, Susannah pushed through the door. Would she need money for bail? At the desk, another officer was in Little Junior's place; the woman lifted the phone receiver and stabbed at the numbers with a pen. She spoke a few words, then pointed to a bench without looking up. "Have a seat." Susannah's stomach churned as she and Bitsy sat. After a few minutes, a door opened and Police Chief Randy Laughton appeared. He motioned to her, and she went over to the door with Bitsy in tow.

"Just you," he said, nodding at Susannah. Bitsy sat down.

Randy ushered Susannah past a row of desks to his office on the other side of the building. Holding the door for her, he let her into his office and shut the door. Two chairs were situated in front of his desk, and he motioned to them. Susannah sat, clutching her purse. The chief's office was cozier than she would have expected.

She cleared her throat. "Where's Angie?"

"I'll get to that." At his desk, he stabbed at a button on his phone and said a few words into the receiver. He hung up and turned to Susannah. "We need to ask you some questions."

"I already gave my statement about Gus." Susannah swallowed. Being here gave her a lump in her throat.

CHAPTER SEVEN

"This is about your sister." Randy hooked his thumbs over his belt. His gray-blue eyes and short light hair stood out against his rosy complexion. He fixed her with his best law enforcement stare.

Susannah's face fell. "I don't understand. What is she being charged with?"

"She's not being charged," Randy replied.

There was a tap on the door, and Detective Varina Withers entered. She nodded at Susannah. "Dr. Shine."

Susannah looked from the detective to Randy and then back. "What's going on?"

"Where were you this afternoon, Doctor?" the detective asked. She stood against the doorjamb, her hands in the front pockets of her khakis.

"Me? I was at my office seeing patients."

"And after that?"

"Bitsy and I went shopping at America's Finest."

"When did you see your sister last?"

"What's going on?" Susannah protested. "I'm not answering any more of your questions until you tell me what's going on."

Detective Withers glanced at Randy, and he nodded at her, pointing to the empty chair. "Let's have a chat." Detective Withers sauntered to the chair and placed it opposite Susannah. "We found your sister at Gus Arnold's house this afternoon."

"What?" Susannah paused, perplexed. She knew something was going on in Angie's mind. But why had she gone to Gus's house? How did she know where he lived? "What was she doing there?"

"That would be my question to you." Detective Withers leaned back in her chair.

"How would I know?" Shaking her head, Susannah replayed

the morning's conversation with Angie, trying to make sense of the situation. "As far as I know, they aren't acquainted. I barely know him."

"He is a patient of yours, isn't he?" Randy leaned forward in his chair, his flat-top crew cut accusing her of misdeeds.

Susannah inhaled remembering Gus's friendly smile. "Yes, but I've only seen him a few times." She straightened her spine and looked him in the eye. "Never outside the office. I have no idea where he lives."

"Well, your sister does." Randy steepled his fingers. "Susannah, we don't want to get off on the wrong foot with this investigation. That's why we're asking for your cooperation."

"I've always been cooperative. But I can't help you." Susannah stood. She was done with their pointless questions. Either they explained themselves, or she was gone. "I don't know why Angie would have gone to Gus's house. I don't even know how she found out where he lives. She must have been curious about his death. It's not a crime to be outside someone's house, is it?"

"She wasn't outside his house. She was inside the house," Randy said.

Susannah sat. This was worse than she had thought. How did Angie get into Gus Arnold's house? As she dug her fingernails into the faux-leather armrests of the chair, her next question came out in a whisper: "She broke into his house?"

"She didn't break in." Detective Withers sat up and leaned forward, her brows pulled down, that serpentine visage back. "She let herself in."

"You mean the door was open?"

"No," Randy said. "She had a key."

CHAPTER EIGHT

In One Chamber and Out the Other

Susannah looked from Randy to Detective Withers and back. "She had a key?" Neither of them said anything.

Thanks to her days in law enforcement, Susannah knew that silence was a tactic used to pressure someone to speak. It usually worked well. Her palms began to sweat, but she said nothing. There was nothing she could say. She could think of no logical reason why Angie would have a key to Gus's house. But there had to be one. Glancing away from the detective, she racked her brain for something to say. Detective Withers leaned further forward, and a discomfort grew in Susannah's belly—that old familiar alien boring into her gut. Finally, she gave in to the desire to speak. "I have no idea what's going on."

Detective Withers slowly returned to her slouched position, and Randy's shoulders relaxed. Susannah stood. She eyed Randy, someone she had known for years and had grown to dislike more and more over the last few months. "If Angie wasn't arrested, what is she doing here?"

Detective Withers stood and pushed her hands deep into her front pockets, about to say something, but Randy interrupted.

"Your sister was found at the scene of an investigation and could have been charged with interfering with that investigation." Randy gazed at her, his blue-gray eyes resolute.

"Officer Chaffin saw her enter the premises." Detective Withers made eye contact with Susannah as if daring her to contradict, maintaining that serpentine expression. "He took her into custody before she had a chance to touch anything."

Randy moved around the desk. "Legally, it's not trespassing because she had a key."

"She claims Gus gave her the key so she could let herself in," Detective Withers continued. "And we can't dispute that. But she needs to stay away while this case is still ongoing."

"You both do," Randy said, rapping his knuckles on the desk.

Susannah raised her brows at Randy but didn't take the bait. "Then you have no reason to hold either of us."

Randy gritted his teeth and motioned toward the detective. Susannah turned away from him, stood up, and headed for the door. The detective opened the door and nearly ran into Owen Chaffin, who was passing by. He glanced in and gave Susannah a small nod of greeting. He wore a sympathetic expression, and Susannah was glad that someone was on her side. Detective Withers led Susannah to the same room she had been questioned in a few months before. Angie sat at a table, her hands around a bottle of water. "Suzie!"

"Let's go."

Angie leaped out of her chair, eyes wide. "I—"

Susannah held her hand up. "Don't say anything, I'm not in the mood." She hurried down the hall and out to the waiting area with Angie trailing behind her. On the bench, Bitsy was involved in a game on her phone. Susannah tapped her on the shoulder. "We're outta here."

CHAPTER EIGHT

Bitsy grabbed her purse and followed them out to Susannah's car. "Didn't have to pay bail, I see. That's good."

Susannah mumbled a response to Bitsy, who had taken up her usual position in the front passenger seat. Angie sat in the back, and Susannah twisted her rearview mirror so that she could see her sister. "Where's your car?"

"At Gus's."

"I have to take Bitsy to get her truck at America's Finest. Then we'll go get your car." When they arrived at America's Finest, Susannah pulled into the parking space next to Bitsy's SUV and turned to her. "One of us will come and get Caden once we have Angie's car."

Bitsy tucked her phone into her purse and touched Susannah's arm. "I already spoke to Andrea. She's cooking up a gluten-free roast chicken, just the way you like it. We call it the 'Get Out of Jail Special.'" Andrea had cooked the same meal the evening Bitsy had picked Susannah up from being questioned about a murder. Bitsy shot her a grin, and Susannah managed a smile. Bitsy could make her smile no matter what was happening. "Go easy on her."

"Get out of my car," Susannah playfully told her. "Angie, come and sit up here."

Bitsy waggled her eyebrows and opened the door. Hugging Angie, she pulled her key chain with the peach fob from her purse. "See y'all in a few."

Angie pulled the door closed and sat for a moment looking at her hands. "Don't be mad."

"I don't know if I am mad." Backing out of the space, Susannah looked over her shoulder, avoiding her sister's gaze. "But I sure as heck wasn't going to get into it in front of that detective."

Angie said nothing.

"Where does Gus live?" Susannah drummed her fingers on the steering wheel as she listened to the directions. They rode in silence for a few minutes.

"You're lucky you have such a good friend," Angie said. "She's always there for you."

"That's because she's connected to half the people in the county. Which means she's usually one step ahead of everyone else." Susannah tightened her grasp on the steering wheel. "Why didn't you wake me up when you got home from work last night?"

"Wake you up?"

"Where were you?"

Angie leaned her head against the passenger window. "After work I went to Gus's."

Susannah drew in a sharp breath. The sister she had always looked up to, the mother of her adorable nephew, was sneaking around like a thief in the night. "You were at Gus's? Why?"

Angie sighed, looking out the window into the dark night. "It's a long story."

Susannah blew out a breath. "I've got time."

"I went to get my gun."

CHAPTER NINE

Drive-through Details

"What?" Her fingers trembling, Susannah stopped her drumming. She bit her lip. "Wait." Angie had a nine-millimeter Glock. Hadn't Travis said that Gus was killed by a nine-millimeter weapon? A tingling sensation slid down her back. She looked at her fingers and exhaled slowly. It was impossible to believe that her sister had shot Gus. It simply couldn't be. "Start from the beginning." Her sister had only been in Georgia for two months. This was going to be interesting.

Angie didn't say anything for a minute, and Susannah didn't push her. She glanced in her mirror to check traffic and decided to pull into a McDonald's that shared its parking lot with a Piggly Wiggly supermarket. The conversation would be easier if she didn't have to drive during it. "Talk."

"When you called me—"

"Stop!" Susannah cut her off, startled at how loud her voice was. She inhaled and turned on her car radio, searching for some calming tunes, then thought the better of it and mashed the button to silence it. "I mean the very beginning. How did you meet Gus?"

"Suzie, I don't think you needta know all the details."

"You're dead wrong. I don't know what kind of relationship you had with Gus, and I don't care, but that detective has you in her sights. If you were in his house or in his car"—Susannah shuddered as she realized the implications of her words—"they *will* find out. Just one fingerprint and she will build a case around it."

Angie squinted at her, and Susannah knew an argument was coming. "So, you gonna save me from myself?"

"No, I'm going to help you and my nephew. I thought you'd be more worried about Caden than yourself."

Angie went pale. "I am. I'm trying to protect him."

"So am I," Susannah insisted. "I've lived in this town for fifteen years. I know people who can help you—"

"I'm not one of your patients." Angie threw herself into her seat, like a child digging in her heels. "I don't haveta listen to your lectures."

"I'm not lecturing." Susannah lowered her voice and gripped the wheel instead of strangling her sister. "You know, people around here see me as an authority on certain things."

"Oh yeah, except for the person that tried to kill you."

Susannah gasped. "I, uh—"

"Don't look so shocked. You think we don't know how to use the internet in New York?" She pronounced New York like *Noo Yawk*. "You forget that Pop keeps tabs on Tone and Irma too."

Tone was Anthony Mancuso, Susannah's former partner in the NYPD; Irma was his wife. Susannah's time in law enforcement was a part of her life that she had packed away until Detective Varina Withers had forced her to return to policing mode by naming her a chief suspect in the death of a local business owner over the summer. In order to clear her name, Susannah had incurred the wrath of the actual killer. She had confided in Tone but not her family. Her father and brother were in law enforcement, but it was her mother Susannah was most concerned with. She said the rosary constantly anyway. Would she ever leave the church if she knew Susannah had been in danger?

"Ma?" Susannah asked, alarmed.

"Ma's tougher than you think." Angie relaxed her shoulders, and her lips twitched slightly. "She just waves that rosary around to make you feel guilty."

"Who told Pop? Tone?"

"Irma," Angie said, her voice suddenly low and gravelly. She sounded like she wasn't enjoying Susannah's surprise as much as she thought she would. "She was worried about you."

"And now I'm worried about *you*. If I have to start making phone calls to Brooklyn—"

"All right, all right." Angie held up her hands in defeat. "Don't let's go there. Mom and Pop will freak if they find out I'm involved in something like this. They'll—"

"Then, from the top."

Angie sighed and twisted in the seat to face her sister. Her neck was against the door, and she tipped her head up and looked at the roof of the Jeep, black loops of hair spraying against the window. "I met Gus at back-to-school night, and we hit it off. He was funny and smart. I gave him my number, and we started to text. We got together a couple of times to... you know, have some fun."

"Okay." Susannah was caught between wanting to understand and not wanting lurid details. "How did you manage to keep this from me? Where was Caden?"

Angie looked at Susannah. "A couple of times, Gus had some off-campus meetings, and we met up afterward. Caden was still in school."

"Go on."

"That's it. We met up at his house. He wanted to keep it casual, and so did I."

"By 'casual,' you mean 'hidden'?"

Angie's dark eyes flashed. "I mean 'no strings.' At first, I thought it might turn into a relationship. He was kind, and funny, and really smart. He had a brilliant smile, too. But once I realized what kind of guy he was, I wasn't interested. Okay?"

Susannah was puzzled. "What kind of guy was he?"

"Well, I thought…but now I don't know." Her black eyes brimmed with tears and her voice cracked. "Maybe I coulda helped him."

Susannah instantly felt a mix of sympathy and dread. "How could you have helped him?"

Angie looked directly into Susannah's eyes. "I don't know. At first he seemed like a regular guy. You know. Come home, watch TV, go to bed. He didn't even realize that he was a Ryan Gosling look alike, but cuter." She gave Susannah a thin smile. "Later, I thought he was hooking up with other women, or men even. His phone was always blowing up. He got texts he didn't want me to see, and he never answered the phone when I was around. He always sent his calls to voice mail. I mean, I wasn't interested in getting married, but I didn't want to be one of many, especially if he wasn't going to be honest about it."

"You couldn't have helped him," Susannah said, trying to make sense of Gus's behavior. "You didn't know what was going on."

"I know," Angie said miserably. Her curls mopped the

window. She sighed. "Anyway, it's too late now."

Susannah nodded and glanced at the McDonald's. "I need coffee. You want anything?"

Angie dug around in her shoulder bag, found a tissue, and blew her nose. "I'm coming." She pulled down the visor, dabbed at her eyes with a finger, and applied some new mascara. Sniffing, she threw the tube into her bag.

Susannah got out of the Jeep to stretch her legs. Leaning on the door, she crossed her arms, watching Angie fumble through her shoulder bag in search of something. After a few minutes, Susannah got back in the car. "Let's just drive through." She started the Jeep and circled the parking lot to the McDonald's menu board. The speaker crackled, and Susannah ordered for them, one eye on Angie, who was peering at the contents of her bag with a perplexed expression. Susannah took their order from the window and handed a coffee to Angie, who nodded and placed her shoulder bag on the floor.

"Okay, Ange," Susannah said. "Now tell me about the gun."

CHAPTER TEN

Changing Sites

Susannah removed the cover to her latte, inhaled the aroma, and cautiously tried a sip. Too hot. She replaced the cover and put it into her cup holder. As they exited the parking lot, she looked at Angie. "I'm waiting."

Angie blew on her coffee, looking at Susannah over the cup. "Quit stalling."

"Gus was gonna change the sights on my gun, so I left it with him. That's all." She paused to blow on her coffee again and tentatively took a sip. "He's certified, or whatever, by Glock. So I thought, why not? When you called me, I panicked. I thought if they found my gun there, I would be dragged into the investigation."

"We wouldn't want that, now, would we?" Susannah shot a look at her sister.

"Get off my back, will ya?" Angie tossed her head, shaking her black hair off her shoulders. "I went to get the gun, but I picked up the wrong gun case."

"Are you saying you got in and out of there once before, without the cops knowing?"

"Yeah." She sipped at her coffee. "I thought I could do it

again. I almost made it, too."

"How did you almost make it? Randy told me that Officer Chaffin saw you going in, and you didn't have time to do anything."

"He saw me goin' in the second time."

Susannah clenched the steering wheel. "Clear this up for me. I called you last night and told you about Gus. Then, when you left work, you went to Gus's. Right?"

Angie nodded.

"Then you came home and slept for a while."

"I never really slept."

Susannah felt her blood pressure rising. "But you came back home and went into your room and closed the door like you were sleeping. I took Caden to school, and you got up and decided to make lasagna."

"I never did make the lasagna. You were right about that."

"Then you drove back to Gus's and decided to go back into a crime scene?"

"Don't yell at me, Suzie! I didn't know it was a crime scene. You told me ya found him"—her voice got thicker as she choked back tears—"at the school. I wasn't thinking straight. I'm just trying to protect Caden."

"Hmmm." Susannah didn't want to interrupt her, but she thought that if her sister really was worried about protecting Caden, she wouldn't have been hooking up with someone she didn't know or trust.

"I thought if I got my gun outta his house, there would be no way to connect us."

"Well, now they'll be looking for ways to connect you." Susannah felt a stab of stomach pain as she remembered how persistent Detective Withers could be.

"I know, I know," Angie said miserably. "Don't remind me."

"But why did you go back in?"

"I was in such a rush to leave that I forgot my keys. I thought I threw them in my pocketbook," she pronounced *pocketbook* like *pokkabook*, a Brooklyn-ism Susannah hadn't heard in years. She tried not to cringe. "I must have dropped them at some point."

Susannah eyed her sister. Something didn't sound right. Angie's leather shoulder bag was like a black hole at her side. Everything that got near her was sucked into the bottom of it. Susannah had seen her toss things in there without realizing she was doing it. She found herself wondering if that was what really happened in Gus's house.

They drove the rest of the way without speaking except for the occasional direction Angie provided. As they got closer, Susannah understood why Officer Chaffin had spotted Angie so easily. Gus's property was set back off a secondary road. His front yard was about half an acre of lawn with nothing to catch the eye. No flower beds or bushes to hide behind, just flat and clear. There was no curb, and a shallow ditch ran along the road, preventing cars from parking there. A large oak tree, whose roots reached down into the ditch, stood at the edge of his driveway, but nothing could have concealed Angie's car sitting in the driveway. Susannah pulled into the driveway and parked behind Angie's car. She looked at her sister and sighed.

"You sure you have your keys now?"

Angie nodded and began digging through her bag.

"Good. Then how about telling me what really happened, and we'll never speak of it again."

Angie stopped, her hands frozen in place. "What do you

CHAPTER TEN

mean?"

Susannah watched her sister chew her lip, a habit Angie normally covered up with copious amounts of lipstick. Tonight, her lower lip showed some damage from biting. "I mean, I don't believe you. You're leaving something out."

Before Angie could speak, blue flashing lights appeared in the rearview mirror. Susannah twisted to look behind her. A familiar voice came across the loudspeaker: "Get out of the car with your hands up."

Susannah shot a glance at Angie, who had raised her hands but was not moving. Slowly opening her door, Susannah stepped out and faced Randy Laughton, who stood outside his cruiser with the microphone for the public address speaker in his hand. The passenger door of the Jeep opened, and Angie stepped out.

"Hands in the air," Randy said through the speaker. Both women complied. Randy put the microphone back in the car as Detective Withers got out of the cruiser's passenger side. Removing his handcuffs from his belt, Randy strode toward Angie with the detective behind him. He took her hands and pulled them down behind her back. "You're under arrest for the murder of Gus Arnold."

CHAPTER ELEVEN

Camp-O-Ween

Susannah shifted on the air mattress and stared up at the inside of the tent while Bitsy snored softly beside her. Jamal and Caden had enjoyed their weekend so much that she had heard them chattering excitedly about the next camp-out. Maggie Hibbard's sons were in their group, but Maggie kept to herself, except for when she was nagging Travis. A long day hiking trails, and an evening making s'mores over a campfire, had led to Jamal and Caden collapsing in an exhausted heap inside their tent. Even Noah, one of the older boys whose tent was close by, was in early and asleep fast.

Grateful that Caden hadn't asked about Angie, Susannah could hardly believe two days had passed since Angie had been arrested. Susannah replayed every second of the arrest in her mind multiple times per day. Randy, crewcut and steely-eyed, the blue lights on his light-bar flashing. Detective Withers, awful eyes with their serpentine squint bearing down on her sister. Angie's tears as she looked to Susannah for help. But it was too late. Angie's gun had been found at the crime scene, they claimed. That was that. Later, Susannah had found the Glock case underneath the seat in Angie's car, and her heart leapt. *Maybe there's been a mistake!*

But it was empty.

Angie had taken the wrong case, an empty case, out of Gus's house. What did that mean? Was Angie lying? Or had someone stolen her gun from Gus's house and used it to kill him?

Susannah sighed and rolled over, peering out the mesh window at the pine trees. The air mattress undulated with each of Bitsy's exhalations. Susannah heard the sound of a zipper in the quiet of the morning, then the rustle of a camper leaving his cocoon. In a moment, Caden was outside her tent, his face scrunched against the mesh of the door. "I have to go potty, but I don't want the monsters to get me." He squatted and began to unzip the door, then stopped. "It's stuck."

Susannah rolled off the air mattress and hit the ground with a grunt. The wave she created tossed Bitsy onto her side, and the snoring momentarily ceased. Peering at the door, Susannah noticed that the fluffy bits from Bitsy's pink slipper had been zipped up in the door. "Hang on," she said to Caden as she wiggled the slipper and tugged on the mechanism.

"There are monsters in the woods," another voice groaned from the window at the side of the tent. "Noah told us to stay inside the tent or the monsters will get us, but I have to use the restroom."

Bitsy pushed her sleep mask onto her forehead and sat up. "Jamal, you get your face outta that window. You gonna ruin my brand new camp-out tent." She bumped to the edge of the mattress and leaned over Susannah's shoulder. "Go easy now," she said. "Don't break that zipper with your spine-crushing chiropractic hands."

Susannah threw a look at Bitsy and tugged with such momentum that she fell back into her friend's lap as tiny bits of pink fluff filled the air. She dropped the slipper and crawled through the opening, pulling Caden in to her. "It's okay. I can take you to the latrine." She upended her hiking boots, which had spent the night outside, and banged them, making sure no stinging critters were inside.

Jamal appeared from around the tent. "I don't want to go the latrine. Auntie Bitsy said I could get tick-bit there. I want to go to the dining hall restroom," Jamal said.

Susannah pulled her hoodie down and stamped her feet. The October air was sharp. What time was it? "Fine, fine," she said, looking around the campsite, hoping one of the male leaders were awake. If they were, they were smart enough to stay bundled inside their sub-zero-rated sleeping bags.

Bitsy yawned as she emerged from the tent. "I could use the restroom too."

Susannah walked the boys to their tent and peered inside, locating and picking up Caden's hoodie. "Where is Noah?" She helped Caden put the heavy garment over his pajama top.

"I don't know," Caden mumbled from inside the fleece.

"Did he already go to the dining hall?" She glanced around the campsite. The campfire ring was deserted, portable canvas chairs vacant. The small pavilion was empty and the woods were silent. The trail to the dining hall was barely visible, but no one was around for yards in any direction. She yawned and felt around in her pocket for her phone. Six twenty-five a.m. Maybe she could wheedle a nice strong cup of coffee out of one of the kitchen staff before breakfast officially started at seven.

"I don't know, he wouldn't tell us," Jamal said, holding up a sneaker. "Found it."

"He told us to stay in the tent or the monsters would get us,"

CHAPTER ELEVEN

Caden said, his voice a scratchy whisper. "So we did. And then I fell asleep."

Susannah bent, peering into the boys' tent again. No sign of Noah. She wasn't sure if she should be alarmed or angry. "Let's go."

Bitsy led the way up the steep path to the dining hall in silence. When they reached the top of the hill, Susannah paused, out of breath from the climb. The dining hall was a large, squat building, one of the few buildings on the grounds of the camp. At the far corner of the dining hall, not far from a group of scout leaders, a man stood smoking.

"There's Mr. Travis." Jamal pointed, then sprinted past the thirty-foot flagpole and across the flat, grassless area in front of the dining hall. The hunched figure of Travis Keene, clad in jeans and a denim jacket, darted around the corner. Caden followed Jamal, passing a group of uniformed troop leaders, heads together, talking. "Mr. Travis!" Jamal called.

"Boys! Come back." Susannah waved at their backs.

The troop leaders looked askance as Bitsy sped past them, the laces of her hiking boot slapping the ground. She caught the boys before they scampered around the corner. Susannah huffed, catching up to her. She peered around the corner. Travis was gone. "Holy cow," Susannah puffed, hands on her knees. "When did I get so out of shape?"

"Around the same time Angie started feeding you trays of gluten-free lasagna."

Susannah pinched an area of fat around her waist and shook her head. "Did you see anything?"

"No. Maybe it wasn't Travis." Bitsy pointed at the open door to the kitchen, from which steam escaped. "Maybe it was one of the cooks."

Susannah shook her head. She was sure it was Travis. Glancing down, she saw a cigarette butt. She nudged Bitsy with her elbow and pointed at the butt with her toe. "Why don't you take the boys to the restroom, and I'll poke around here for a minute."

As they turned to go, Susannah squatted to snap a picture with her phone. The brand was Camel, the same brand she had seen tucked behind Travis's ear at the store. Next to it, she noticed the deep impression of a heel in the soft earth—a print that could have been made by a cowboy boot. From the open door, a man stared at her as he dumped water out of a plastic basin onto the ground. That accounted for the softness of the soil on this side of the building. Scanning the area, she noted another cigarette butt, a Marlboro, and took a picture of that. The prints of other hiking boots and sneakers were not so deep. Directly across from Travis's print there was the impression of a smaller hiking boot with a very distinctive, three-pronged design in the middle of the tread. Susannah tapped her phone and made several images, then turned to go. There was the snap of a twig and she spun around, but all she saw was a fluffy-tailed squirrel scurrying up a tree.

At the entrance of the dining room, scents of coffee and bacon floated out to greet her. Bitsy stood with her hands on her hips before a closed door; she blew out a sigh of frustration and pounded on the door. The noise echoed through the trees, and one of the scout leaders peered around the corner of the building at them.

"The dining hall's not open yet," he said and disappeared.

"Hmmph," Bitsy replied, raising her fists to knock again when the door opened with a scraping sound. Noah Howard stared at them.

CHAPTER ELEVEN

"Noah," Susannah said, surprised. "What are you doing here?" Noah's face went red as he looked from Susannah to Bitsy to the boys.

"I'm sorry I had to leave the boys," he sputtered. "But Mr. Travis needed me for breakfast duty."

"Where is Mr. Travis?" Susannah asked, craning her neck to look past him into the dim hall.

"I don't know." Noah's body twitched; Susannah thought he was hiding something.

Bitsy stepped into the doorway, but Noah didn't move. "I'm not allowed to let anyone in yet."

Bitsy clucked at him. "Those rules are for the boys, not grown ladies in need." She raised her eyebrows at him, and he took a step back, giving her ample room to barrel past him into the building, pulling Jamal along behind her.

Susannah pushed Caden in. "Go with Miss Bitsy." She touched Noah on the sleeve. "Does Mr. Keith know you're here?"

Noah swallowed and looked over his shoulder toward the kitchen. "I don't want to get Mr. Travis in trouble," he whispered. "I wasn't supposed to be on kitchen duty, but he woke me up and told me to get my butt out and come with him. So I did."

"Where did he go?"

"He was in the kitchen at first. Got him a cup of coffee and then"—he lowered his voice—"was smoking outside the kitchen door. Miss Maggie's gonna get onto him about it if she finds out. He thought I didn't see him, but I did."

A bad feeling niggled at Susannah's gut. Could Travis be somehow tangled up with Gus's death? First Gus was shot, and Travis said he knew Gus had been shot with a nine-millimeter gun, then Angie was framed. Susannah inhaled and felt a sharp pain under her ribs. She hoped to God that Angie *was* being framed. Her sister had a lot of faults, but murdering her clandestine boyfriends was not one of them. She tapped her upper lip, thinking. Did Travis know Gus? Gus was new to town, but Peach Grove was small, and Travis owned a busy shop. Like Bitsy, he probably had contacts all over the county.

A yank on her arm made her jump. Caden looked up at her. She had been so deep in thought she hadn't heard the boys approach. "When do we eat, Aunt Suzie?" asked Caden.

"Y'all need to get out of that doorway and line up with your troop." A gruff voice bellowed from outside the building. Susannah turned to see a uniformed man wearing a Smokey the Bear hat, glaring at her. In his hands, he clutched a clipboard. "What troop are you with?"

Caden grabbed Jamal's hand, and they both looked up at the man, speechless. Susannah approached and said, "They're with me."

The man narrowed his eyes at her. "The dining hall is not open until seven. No food is served until after all troops check in and we say the Pledge of Allegiance."

"I—"

A loud ruckus came from within the kitchen as Bitsy stepped through the door, beaming. She held two small blue enamel coffee mugs and quickly crossed the room, her laces slapping on the floor. Mr. Smokey the Bear Hat stared as she exited the building, bringing the smell of coffee with her. She managed to step daintily in her clunky Merrell boots and handed Susannah one of the steaming cups.

The smell of fresh coffee made Susannah want to sing. "How did you get these?" she whispered while watching Bitsy drink.

"Oh, shoo," Bitsy replied. "My second cousin Fanny Vincent-Long has been running this here kitchen"—she aimed a thumb over her shoulder—"since the nineties."

Susannah raised her cup to Mr. Smokey the Bear, who stomped away. Blowing on the hot liquid, the small enamel cup warm in her hand, Susannah sipped at her coffee. She worried about her sister sitting in the Peach Grove jail, waiting on her arraignment. Scanning the paths and woods around her, she wondered if Travis Keene held some answers.

CHAPTER TWELVE

Makeup to Breakup

Susannah flopped down on the couch. The weekend had been harder on her than it had been on Caden. She and Bitsy had kept Caden busy at the camp-out and the *after camp-out* on Sunday afternoon—which was what Bitsy called hanging out in Susannah's living room, with her feet up on the coffee table, watching TV, and eating cold Burger King French fries. Caden and Jamal had played with Legos and then fallen asleep, sprawled across Susannah's sofa. Their dirty jackets were still strewn over a pile of gear Susannah had lugged in from the Jeep.

This morning, Susannah had taken Caden to school, chatting him up to convince him his mom had been working all weekend. He had bought it. Susannah felt a familiar twinge in her stomach. Maybe lying to a seven-year-old wasn't the best parenting strategy, but she couldn't tell her nephew that his mom had been arrested on suspicion of murder.

Susannah pondered her sister's predicament. Angie was in deep trouble. Worse, the bail had been set higher than she'd expected, and a bond on Susannah's house would be needed to secure Angie's release. Hiring a lawyer was now on Susannah's to-do list—after she talked to her sister.

After the arraignment, and an hour's wait, she was able to speak to Angie in jail. "Tell me everything."

"You know most of it." Angie lifted one shoulder. Dark circles under her eyes were enhanced by smudges of eyeliner.

"Tell me *all* of it. How can I help you if I don't know all of it?"

"I think I need a lawyer to help me." Angie ran her hand through her hair, looking off into the distance.

"I'll work on that when I get home."

"Okay." Angie leaned forward. "But you have to believe me. I didn't kill Gus, and no one can get me to say I did. Not even that detective with the squint-eyes."

"I know that," Susannah said, but a feeling of relief spread through her. Was it that she knew for sure that Angie was innocent? Or was it because her sister would finally fill in the missing pieces? "Spill."

"My gun wasn't the only thing I was looking for at Gus's."

Susannah had to keep herself from shouting, *I knew it!* Angie *had* been holding back something—she could read her sister better than anyone else in the world. "What else were you looking for?"

"My lipstick."

Susannah blinked. She wasn't sure she heard her correctly. "Your…"

"My lipstick. The last time I saw Gus, I had Marvelous Magenta with me. I must have dropped it, and I think the police have it."

Susannah's heart was racing. Angie's Marvelous Magenta was custom made for her. "What makes you think that?"

"The kind of questions they were asking me. The same ones,

over and over. I had to tell them."

Susannah was speechless. Slowly a picture formed in her mind: Angie looking pale, Angie pawing through her bag, Angie chewing on her lip. She wasn't pale—she just wasn't wearing lipstick. Other pieces fell into place. According to Little Junior, a woman had left something in Gus's car.

Angie had been in Gus's car!

Susannah reached for Angie's arm, but a guard took a step toward her. "No touching."

"You were in Gus's car before he died?" Susannah whispered.

Angie hung her head. "You gotta believe me, Suzie. I had no idea what Gus was mixed up in. I went by the school to break it off, I swear."

"Why was his car in the parking lot of the library?"

"I don't know. He told me to meet him there. I thought he was leaving his car there to make room for the parents coming to the Fall Festival. I got into his car, but we only talked for a minute. Then I left."

"You had to use your lipstick?"

"Gus took the breakup badly." She pouted at Susannah, and the effect was unnerving. "You know I primp when I'm nervous."

Susannah cleared her throat. "Well, your primping has gotten you here." She couldn't imagine what to do next, but she had to give her sister some hope. "And somehow, I'm going to get you out."

CHAPTER THIRTEEN

Dinner with the Doc

Susannah stroked Rusty as she considered everything she had learned in the last day. Angie had a secret romance with a man who had been murdered. She had been in his car shortly before the murder and in his house shortly afterward, and her gun had been found at the scene of the crime.

It had been a long day for Susannah, starting with her spending the morning at the Peach Grove Judicial Center, and ending with several hours on her feet treating patients. Tina and Larraine bustled around, trying to keep the tone light as they prepared the table for the food arriving soon. "My feet hurt," said Susannah.

"I'm so hungry"—Tina looked over to Susannah—"that I could eat that cat."

Susannah smiled at Tina's attempt to cheer her. She wanted to go home and collapse into her bed, but supper with the ladies was in order. She needed their help.

There was a squeal of brakes, and Tina pushed the curtain to the side. "It's Bitsy."

Susannah was surprised to see Bitsy in the rear parking lot

since it had not been officially exorcised.

Larraine joined them. "Well, thank the Lord. Not a Krispy Kreme or Dairy Queen bag in sight."

"Mrow," Rusty said as he rubbed against Larraine's leg.

She opened the door, and Rusty streaked out past Bitsy, who carried a large shopping bag in one hand and a tray of drinks in the other. Bitsy barreled through the doorway clutching the cardboard tray so firmly that her orange-painted nails made dimples in it. She deposited the food on the table and dropped her shoulder bag on the floor and shuddered. "I felt a spirit pass me by. It put a chill into my bones."

Tina grinned up at her and gently removed her fingers from the cardboard carrier. "It was Rusty. Larraine just let him out."

"Hmmph. That wasn't no feline energy. That there parking lot's been a poltergeist playground for months."

"Close the door." Larraine crossed her arms and pulled her sweater closed.

"Yes, ma'am." Bitsy leaned in. "You felt it too?"

"What I felt was a draft." Larraine shooed her and unloaded the bags.

"Mmm, Mexican food?" Susannah pulled out a white waxy paper bag filled with tortilla chips, which she poured onto a plate. "Thanks for picking up dinner."

"Don't thank me." Bitsy helped Susannah unpack the rest of the food. "Thank Andrea." She took a chip and snapped it in half. "She found me while I was taking down Larraine's demands, um, I mean, dietary restriction list, and suggested Mexican food. She even called in the order for me, gluten-free *enchiladas verdes* and all."

"That's good for Dr. Shine," Tina said as she sat next to Susannah, rubbing her belly. "Well, where do we start? This

CHAPTER THIRTEEN

whole thing has gotten me tied up in knots. Who would shoot someone right outside an elementary school?" She rubbed her arms vigorously. "It's ghoulish."

Bitsy patted Tina's shoulder. "You need to stop parking in that back lot too."

Tina smiled at Bitsy and picked up her fork. "Keith has been closed-mouthed about this whole thing." She pushed some rice around her plate. "But something's different than before," she said, dipping her chin toward Susannah. They all understood her meaning. *Before* meant earlier this summer, when Susannah had been under suspicion of murder.

"I think we have to consider that Gus was not as innocent as he seemed." Susannah swallowed, her appetite gone. Angie certainly wasn't as innocent as Susannah had thought. "Angie mentioned that he got a lot of phone calls and texts that he didn't take when she was around. She thought he was seeing someone else. But maybe he was mixed up with something bad. And maybe Travis was too."

"Why do you say that, Dr. Shine?" asked Tina.

"Because Travis Keene was acting odd over the weekend." Susannah filled them in about his "sources" for knowing about Gus's death and about finding Travis at the dining hall. "The more I think of it, the more suspicious his behavior seems. He was meeting someone there on the sly. I know it."

Before anyone could comment, Bitsy's phone toned and she held up a finger while she answered the call. "Uh-huh, uh-huh," she said, her eyes wide. Her finger wavered as she tapped the screen to end the call. "Y'all are not going to believe this. Travis never came home from the camp-out last night. Little Junior just took Maggie's missing persons report."

"Missing?" Tina's eyes were wide.

"According to Little Junior, his truck is not at the campground."

"Did Gus and Travis know each other?" Larraine asked. Tina shook her head to say *I don't know*. Susannah lifted one shoulder in a halfhearted shrug.

"Little Junior said the same thing yesterday," Bitsy chimed in, lifting a chip covered with jack cheese and jalapeños to her mouth. "About things being more complicated, I mean. He said there's a lot of phone calls going back and forth to the county lately."

"The county?" Larraine fingered the faux pearls on her eyeglass chain.

"Yeah," Bitsy said, cheese dotting her chin. "They have these task forces where the county and the city police combine forces. You know, like a superhero Mod Squad."

Tina spilled some rice off her fork as she giggled. "Miss Bitsy, you crack me up."

Bitsy waggled her eyebrows. "Y'all know what I mean."

"But why?" Susannah asked.

"Well, the task forces work on things that overlap jurisdictions. Like drug deals or illegal gun sales," Tina said, laying her fork down. "And there's one thing we haven't talked about yet."

"What's that?"

"You didn't hear a gunshot, Dr. Shine. The killer might have used a silencer."

Susannah dropped her fork, which clattered loudly on her plate. "That's good news for Angie! She wouldn't know how to find a silencer. If only she had kept hold of her lipstick!"

The three women stared at Susannah. Tina asked, "What about Angie's lipstick?"

CHAPTER THIRTEEN

"Remember how Keith told you the police thought Gus was meeting someone before the Fall Festival?" Susannah asked.

Tina nodded, wide-eyed.

"That someone was Angie."

CHAPTER FOURTEEN

Sour Cream and Choosing Teams

"Angie was the one meeting Gus?" Larraine's fair complexion pinked. "Well, I'll be."

"I didn't see that comin'," Bitsy said, layering beans and rice on a tortilla chip and popping it into her mouth.

"I wish you wouldn't have told me this." Tina got up from her chair with a pained expression. The gold flecks that highlighted her brown eyes shone. "How am I going to keep it from Keith? What if he asks me what we talked about? You know I can't lie to him."

Susannah touched Tina's hand. "They already know."

"I guess Keith is better at keeping things from me than I thought." Tina sat down, her long fingers twisting her wedding ring. Larraine patted Tina's shoulder and then picked up her plate and headed into the kitchen.

"We know Angie was with Gus before he was killed." Susannah sipped her drink, the corners of her mouth turned down. "She says she didn't see anything."

"We have a lot to organize." Larraine stood in the doorway of the kitchen, arms folded, leaning on the doorjamb.

"I have no doubt Gus's murder and Travis's disappearance

are connected," Susannah continued. "We have to connect Gus and Travis."

"Miss Larraine is right, we have to get organized." Bitsy removed the fork from her mouth and shook it at Susannah. "We need two teams. Team Travis and Team Gus."

"Then you're on Team Gus," Susannah said, pointing at her friend, who leaned halfway out of her chair to sift through a tote bag she had left by the door. With a thumbs-up, Bitsy pulled two white paper bags from the tote, one of which was crumpled and stained. "Uh," Susannah said watching her, "you focus on Peach Grove Elementary School."

"Righto." Bitsy unrolled the neck of one paper sack and removed a round take-out container. On top of the aluminum container sat two small plastic condiment cups; one filled with a black liquid and one filled with white liquid. The women watched as she grabbed the bag and ripped it in half. "Anyone got a pen?"

Tina handed her a pen, and Bitsy wrote *Team Gus* on one side of the bag and *Team Travis* on the other. "Okay, Gus was new to town. At the Fall Festival, Eberly Braswell mentioned Gus had taught in Tussahaw Junction before he got promoted to assistant principal in Peach Grove."

"Start by giving Eberly a call," Susannah told Bitsy, "and pump her for more details about Gus." Bitsy stuck the tip of her tongue out and wrote *grill Eberly* on the *Team Gus* bag.

"Miss Larraine?" Tina asked.

"Gus never joined my church." The Peach Grove Baptist Church was the largest congregation in town, and Larraine knew almost every member by name.

Bitsy wrote *heathen* on the bag under *Team Gus*. Susannah opened her mouth to object, but Bitsy placed her pen on the table, grabbed the take-out container, and quickly pulled off the lid. She removed a brown cylindrical stick and then opened one of the condiment cups and dipped it into a black, viscous liquid, then bit off the end.

"What *is* that?" Tina wrinkled her nose as Bitsy dipped the other end into the cup filled with the white sauce.

"Is that sour cream?" Larraine interrupted, squeezing one eye closed, clearly confused at what she was watching.

"Sour cream on churros?" Bitsy asked. She popped the last bit of churro into her mouth, chewing contentedly. "It's whipped cream and chocolate sauce."

"Oh," Susannah and Tina said simultaneously and relievedly.

Bitsy picked up her pen and looked at the women, who stared back at her. "What's wrong?"

"Nothing at all." Larraine crossed her arms. "Where were we?"

"Building Team Gus," Susannah replied. "He didn't go to your church. Does he have family around here?" Tina shrugged. Larraine shook her head to indicate that she didn't know. Susannah turned to Bitsy. "Well, it looks like you and I are on Team Gus. You talk to Eberly. It should be easy to find out what school he worked at in Tussahaw Junction. We need to know about his past. I know he mentioned he was in the military. That's how he hurt his knee."

"I'll see if Roman can help." Bitsy looked hopeful, and then her face drooped. "We would need to know what branch of the military he was in."

Susannah looked at Tina. "You're going to have to see what information you can get out of Keith. You know, not crime-related. Next of kin. Where they live. I'll get on Google and see what I can find." Susannah steepled her fingers. "In fact,

CHAPTER FOURTEEN

Angie told me that Gus had some kind of certification with Glock. He was going to change the sights on her gun. Maybe we can work that angle. He must have known Travis."

"Building Team Travis." Bitsy underlined his name twice. "Miss Larraine, whatcha got?"

Despite the fact that she despised gossip and innuendo, Larraine Moore was a fantastic sleuth, managing to ferret out information from even the most closed-mouthed individual. "Travis and his wife, Crystal, used to attend regular as clockwork. But after they separated, neither have been back."

"How long ago was that?"

"About a year."

Susannah watched Bitsy write *lapsed Baptist* under Travis's column.

"Do you think Crystal might want to have a chat with you?" Susannah looked at Larraine. "You could invite her for a nice sit-down with some of your famous cookies."

"I might could do that." Larraine tugged at her cardigan. "Though she wasn't the most pleasant person to be around. Smokes like a chimney too."

"So does Travis," Susannah commented. "I can go with you. We'll have to come up with some reason to contact her."

Larraine pressed her lips together. Susannah took that as a yes. To Bitsy, she said, "You getting all this?"

Bitsy looked up from doodling devil horns above Crystal Keene's name. "Who, me?"

"What about Maggie Hibbard?" Tina asked. "Anyone need a wash and cut?"

"Put a new 'do' on my list." Larraine stood up, patting her hair. "Maggie and the boys are members, and I reckon I've sent twenty customers her way. Does that make me Team Travis or Team Gus? Her boys go to Peach Grove Elementary too."

Bitsy shook her pen in Larraine's direction.

"Now, ladies, no turf wars." Tina's belly bounced as she laughed.

Susannah checked her watch. "Okay, we have a lot to do." She put up one finger. "Bitsy and I will start with Gus. Bitsy will contact her PTA friends and see what she can learn there. Tina, you also need to find out what Keith knows about Travis's disappearance."

"Wheedling will commence," Tina giggled.

"I'll do some internet searching," said Susannah.

"Meanwhile," Larraine said, "I'll make a call to Maggie about a hair appointment."

"Okay, I think we have a plan."

As her friends left, Susannah pulled Larraine aside. "I'm going to need an attorney for Angie."

"I thought as much." Larraine handed Susannah a business card: Buchanan, Hinton, and Norris. Winston Norris was related to Larraine's son by marriage. The law firm had the reputation of being the toughest one in the county. "Winston will help you get to the truth."

Susannah wondered if she was ready for the truth.

CHAPTER FIFTEEN

Lipsticks and Ballistics

Susannah was elbow deep in sudsy water when a loud knock startled her out of her reverie. She dried her arms and hands with a dish towel as she peered through the peephole of her front door.

After she opened the door, Bitsy leaned forward and stuck her head inside and asked, "You okay?"

"I'm fine. What's going on?"

"I've been callin' and textin'." She peered into Susannah's face and lowered her voice. "Blink if you're in danger."

Susannah laughed. "Come on in. I've been running water and cleaning up the kitchen. I didn't hear the phone."

Bitsy took a step and stopped. "What do I smell—Italian comfort cooking?"

"I think you could say that."

Susannah shut the door and ushered Bitsy into the kitchen as Caden came scampering into the room, naked. "Who's at the door? Is it for me?" he called. He stopped when he saw Bitsy. "Did you bring Jamal? He said he would come over to play."

Bitsy shook her head. "Sorry, sweet pea, it's too late for Jamal to come over. It's a school night."

"But you're here on a school night? Why can't Jamal come too?"

"Because he's probably in bed," Susannah directed Caden to the bathroom and threw a towel around him. "Dry off and get dressed. Then you can come out."

In the kitchen, Bitsy had taken a seat. Susannah asked, "Why *are* you here on a school night?"

"I heard from Eberly, and I heard from Little Junior. He gave me some good news and some less good news." Bitsy raised one eyebrow. "This is not on the record."

"Go on."

"First, Little Junior thinks the item left in Gus's car wasn't a tube of lipstick. It was a cigarette butt with lipstick on it."

"Another woman was in the car with Gus?" Susannah gasped.

"That's not all." Bitsy tapped a nail on the table. "Little Junior thinks the ballistics report will clear Angie once they release it."

"That *is* good news." Biting her lip, Susannah asked the obvious. "When are they going to release it?"

"They're not." Picking up one of Susannah's wonky gluten-free blueberry muffins, Bitsy nibbled at it. "Leastways not yet. Eventually, they'll have to. But for now, they're keeping it quiet."

"Why?" Susannah took the muffin from Bitsy's hand, broke it in half, and popped a piece into her own mouth.

"I don't want to say it's a cover-up, but let's say Detective Westers has her mind set on Angie."

Susannah didn't correct her friend's mispronunciation of Varina Withers's name. "How sure is Little Junior about this?"

"His information is usually spot on." Bitsy lifted her hands.

CHAPTER FIFTEEN

"But he's worried that they won't release the report. Nothing is a hundred percent until he sees it in writing."

Susannah put her finger to her lips. They heard a door close, and Caden appeared in the living room. "Come and say good night to Miss Bitsy."

Caden hugged Bitsy. "Good night."

Susannah put her arm around her nephew. "Get into bed, and I'll come and read you a story." Caden nodded and scampered off. Susannah turned to Bitsy. "We have to get Angie out of jail quick. Caden thinks Angie is away doing some special training for the hospital. I'm not going to be able to keep lying to him. Or to my mother for that matter."

"Just be patient." Bitsy sat up. "I spoke to Eberly. She told me that Gus was in the Marines and was discharged because of his knee injury. She didn't know more than that. I'm gonna meet her for supper tomorrow and see what else I can get out of her. She mentioned that Gus worked at the Tussahaw Junction Elementary School as a teacher. This was his first job as an assistant principal."

Caden called from his room, and Susannah stood. "Right. Let's make some time and go to America's Finest and snoop around."

"How about tomorrow at lunchtime?"

"Sounds like a plan. America won't know what hit them."

CHAPTER SIXTEEN

America's Finest

Susannah parked under the giant American flag that hung over the entryway of Travis Keene's store. America's Finest Sporting Goods was an impressive achievement, and Susannah tried to reconcile that with the man she had seen hanging around outside the dining hall of a boy's camp in the middle of the woods. Something told her he hadn't been there just to sneak a cigarette. But what *had* he been doing? She waved at Bitsy, whose SUV slid into the parking place next to hers, and released the door locks. Bitsy exited her SUV and slipped into the Jeep.

"So, what's the plan?" Bitsy made finger guns and rocked them back and forth.

"We're going to be casual shoppers, that's all," Susannah said. "I have office hours this afternoon, so let's not take a lot of time. Browse around and look for anything out of the ordinary. If you see a sales clerk, ask some questions."

"Like, 'Where is your crazy-ass boss hiding?'" Bitsy nudged her in the ribs. "How's that for casual?"

"A little too casual."

Bitsy used her finger guns again. "Gotcha."

CHAPTER SIXTEEN

"Angie said Gus was certified to work on Glocks. I'm going to go to the gun counter and start up a conversation there, and ask if they have someone who can change the sights on my gun. Maybe they have Gus's name on a list of gunsmiths or something. You check out the shoes and hikers." Susannah pulled up the photo of the hiking bootprint and texted it to Bitsy, whose phone pinged to announce its arrival. "Look for that tread. If we can match it to the prints we saw at the camp, maybe it will tell us something."

"Sure thing." Bitsy opened the door a crack. "Let me go in first. I need a head start on some browsing I want to do for Growl-A-Ween supplies. I also need a new concealed-carry purse. I have a two-pronged angle of attack." She jumped out and ambled into the store.

Susannah tugged on a strand of hair. Could Travis Keene really have murdered Gus? A murder and a disappearance in the same week couldn't be a coincidence. But she needed proof. She waited a little while and then went into the store, where she strolled around the Major League Baseball team caps and came to the aisle she and Bitsy had browsed for ammo. Around the corner, the gun counter was deserted, and Susannah examined the firearms. A small cardboard display sat on the countertop advertising a sale on the Smith & Wesson M&P Shield.

"Can I help you?" A thin woman with stringy blond hair studied her, gaze lingering momentarily on Susannah's shoes. Susannah suddenly felt that she was dressed all wrong. The woman, whose name tag read CRYSTAL, was wearing faded blue jeans, a flannel shirt, and brown hiking boots. Remembering that she was not an accomplished liar, Susannah stammered, "Uh, yeah, I own a Glock and—"

"You own a Glock?" Crystal stepped closer. Tilting her head, she eyed Susannah as if trying to decide if she were telling the truth. "Which one?"

"A 43, and I—"

"Well, that makes some kinda sense. A girly girl like you would get one of them tiny little pocket pistols." Crystal leaned toward Susannah and tapped her shoulder bag. "Is it in there?"

"Uh, no."

"Oh." Crystal grinned, then backed up and nudged Susannah's ankle with the toe of her hiking boot. "You got an ankle holster, then."

"No. I don't have it with me."

"Well, why the heck not?" Crystal's voice got louder and small lines formed in the corners of her eyes. "Why in the world did you buy a subcompact gun designed for concealed carry if you're not going to carry it?"

An employee stepped out from the storeroom behind the display case and gawked at them, then retreated. Susannah opened her mouth to respond, but nothing came out. She hadn't expected to be on the receiving end of a barrage of questions. *She* was supposed to be asking the questions.

"I've asked her that question myself." Bitsy appeared holding two purses and a plastic hanger on which hung a neon-pink sports bra. "We're gonna solve that with these here concealed-carry purses. But we—" She glanced at Crystal's shoes and stopped. "Oh, I like those hiking boots."

Crystal gave Bitsy a sneer. "Well, go buy you a pair."

"No thanks." Bitsy swung the bra hanger on one finger. "But my friend and I were wonderin' if you could recommend someone that works on Glocks? Like Travis maybe?"

Crystal slapped her hand on the glass of the gun display case. Susannah and Bitsy flinched. "Travis? He don't know nothing about foreign-made guns. You see the name of the store? America's Finest. Not Germany's Finest."

This was not at all what Susannah had envisioned.

Crystal continued, "I done told him Remington and Smith & Wesson are solid American gun manufacturers. Why do we need to buy from foreign companies?"

A man wearing a red smock rounded the corner. He wore a tag that read MANAGER.

"Crystal," the manager began, "we've asked you nicely to leave. I'm giving you one more chance to get gone. I called the police, and if you're still here when they arrive—"

"You low-down weasel." Crystal picked up the cardboard display piece and threw it at him. "This here shop is mine as much as it is Travis's. We're still married, and this business is a marital asset."

"Well, you all can take that up in court, for all I care," the manager said, his arm over his head to ward off anything else she might pitch his way. "You're not an employee of this company, and you need to leave."

"Let's go." Susannah grasped Bitsy's hand and headed for the exit, but Bitsy redirected her toward the register.

"We need this stuff."

The concealed-carry handbags were already on the checkout counter and being rung up by the manager when the Peach Grove PD cruiser pulled up. Bitsy gawked at the cruiser through the store's plate glass window as she dropped the pink sports bra over the purses. Officer Chaffin rushed into the store and headed toward the firearms. Exiting the store, bags in hand, Susannah eyed Chief Laughton as he screeched into the lot. He exited his vehicle at a jog, taking in the women. "Ladies." He slowed, narrowing his eyes. "What might the two of you be doing here?"

"We were just leaving." Susannah glanced at her vehicle.

"Interesting." Randy pulled his sunglasses down his nose and peered at Susannah and Bitsy. "A material witness in the death of one citizen found shopping at the store of another citizen who happens to be missing. Susannah, you wouldn't be poking your nose into our investigation, would you?"

Bitsy glanced at Randy as she fished in her shoulder bag for her keys. "There ain't no crime in shopping that I know about."

"I was looking for hiking boots. But"—Susannah gave Randy an innocent shrug—"they didn't have my size."

"I think crazy Crystal got the last pair. That girl's cornbread ain't done in the middle, if you know what I mean." Bitsy gestured toward Randy with her keys, the peach fob swinging. "Isn't that why you're here?" Bitsy removed one of the purses from the shopping bag and threw it to Susannah. "Happy birthday." She jumped into her SUV and slammed the door.

"It's not my—"

As the engine engaged, Bitsy brought her hand up to her face, her finger and thumb a mock phone. *Call me*, she mouthed, then pulled out of the parking space.

"—birthday," finished Susannah

Hands on his gun belt, Randy glared at Susannah. She stared down at her feet, hoping he wouldn't continue the lecture. A shout from inside the store sent him hustling off, and Susannah sighed.

Another day in paradise.

Susannah jumped into her Jeep and drove away.

CHAPTER SEVENTEEN

Cutz & Curlz

Cutz & Curlz, Maggie Hibbard's salon, was housed in a renovated Queen Anne Victorian similar to Bitsy's house, which was located further down Peachtree Street. Extra-large ferns hung under the wraparound porch, and Susannah ducked under one as Maggie waved them in and gave Larraine a hug. "What's all this?"

"Just a little something for the boys." Larraine held up the casserole carrier. Her three-cheese macaroni and cheese was famous around town. "How are you holding up?"

"Oh, Miss Larraine, you didn't have to. It's not like someone died." Her hand flew to her mouth, her eyes wide. "I mean, I'm sure Travis is fine. Excuse me a moment."

Maggie put the carrier down and crossed into a room lined with professional hairdryers with attached padded chairs. A woman under a dryer read a *People* magazine. She waved as Maggie lifted the dryer.

"Isn't that Miss Shirleen?" Susannah asked Larraine.

Larraine peered down her glasses. "Shirleen Carter. My, my." Shirleen, one of Larraine's best friends and a fellow member of the Peach Grove Baptist Church Welcoming Committee, was never far from juicy gossip. Shirleen grinned at Larraine and returned to her magazine.

Maggie waved the women into the back room, where she stored the casserole in a refrigerator. Susannah noticed a plate of Miss Shirleen's pumpkin chocolate chip cookies on a table. Maggie said, "Miss Carter has a few minutes before I have to remove her foils, and I wanted to speak to you in private."

Susannah regarded Maggie. Her face was drawn and worried, but her eyes were clear. She hadn't been crying. Did she know something the police didn't? Susannah slowly lowered herself into a chair that had been pulled up to a scratched wooden table. A few thick glossy magazines nestled next to a pair of hair-thinning scissors. With one blade shaped like a comb, the instrument looked very odd, angled with the handles splayed open.

"I appreciate your prayers and thoughts, Miss Larraine." Maggie closed the door behind her and continued, "But I think Travis is fine."

Larraine tugged her sweater. "Didn't you call him in missing?"

"Well, yes, I did report him missing." She inhaled. "But that's because I was angry."

"Angry?" Larraine asked. "About what?"

Maggie's bottom lip quivered. "I don't think he's missing. I think he left me." She crumpled into a chair. "I've been texting him since we left the campsite Sunday morning. I got one reply." Tears brimmed in her eyes, and she wiped them away. "The rat. I wanted to get back at him for leaving me."

"There, there." Larraine stroked her arm.

Susannah observed Maggie. She appeared genuinely upset. "What did his text say?"

CHAPTER SEVENTEEN

"He said he had to run an errand." Maggie's green eyes flashed, and she clenched her teeth before she blurted, "Ha! Some errand. Probably went sniffin' after his ex. Crystal's some piece of work, that one." She picked up the hair-thinning scissors and waved them around, accentuating her words. Susannah and Larraine leaned away. Maggie's hand—the one without the scissors—flew to her mouth again, her eyes wide. "Oh, Miss Larraine, I am so sorry you had to hear that ugliness."

"What makes you think that?" Susannah asked.

"She lives in Tussahaw Junction, not far from the camp." Maggie sniffed.

Susannah shot a glance to Larraine. Apparently, Maggie did not know that Travis and Crystal were still married, and Susannah wasn't going to give her the news. Larraine played with a button on her sweater.

Maggie said, "You're not going to tell anyone, are you? About the getting back at him part, I mean." A few tears leaked from her eyes, and she grabbed a box of tissues and blew her nose. "What with Crystal living down that way, I don't think it's anything to worry about."

"Don't fret about it," Larraine said. "Relationships can be hard."

"You're right." Maggie dabbed at her face with a clean tissue. "You can imagine what it's like to be a single mom running a business. I don't exactly have time to date. When I met Travis, we both agreed that we didn't want anything serious, but…"

Larraine patted Maggie. "It's going to be okay."

Maggie went on, "I guess he grew on me. And the kids liked him well enough."

"You don't have to explain anything to us, sugar," Larraine said.

"I know, it's just that between his store and his hobbies, and my store and the boys...well, we didn't have much time together. When he agreed to join the scout troop, I thought he was getting serious. That's why I nagged him about the smoking." She picked at the tissue. "I thought if he was going to be around the boys more, you know, it's bad for their health."

"Of course. Secondhand smoke is a real issue." Susannah could imagine Angie yelling at her for being too blunt, and she began to sweat.

"Exactly." Maggie nodded. "I'm glad I didn't build him up to the boys. Get their hopes up that they were getting a stepdad."

Larraine took her by the arm. "It might not be what you think. But either way, we're here for you. Between Miss Shirleen and me, we have half the congregation on speed dial. If you need anything at all, just let us know."

"Thank you, Miss Larraine." Maggie forced a smile, then looked at Susannah. "I almost forgot. I heard you saw Travis Sunday morning at the camp-out."

"Well..." Susannah hesitated. She didn't want to rub salt into the woman's wounds. "It looked like him, but he walked away so fast, I couldn't get a good look."

"What was he doing?"

"He was by himself, smoking."

Maggie let out a peal of laughter. "By himself, smoking? That sounds like Travis."

"If you don't mind me asking," Susannah began, "what brand did he smoke?"

"Filtered Camels."

A buzzer sounded. Maggie tossed her tissues into the trash, nodded at the women, and scurried out of the back room. Giving Miss Shirleen a good-bye wave, Larraine and Susannah

CHAPTER SEVENTEEN

saw themselves out. In the Jeep, Larraine donned her bifocals, grabbed her phone, and shared what they had learned with Bitsy. Then she frowned at her screen.

"Bitsy said to tell you that Crystal's the boot lady." Larraine looked at Susannah over her glasses. "What does that mean, *boot lady?*"

"It means Maggie may be right about Travis."

CHAPTER EIGHTEEN

Graveyard Glimpses

The next morning, Susannah stood behind Larraine at the front desk as she typed the last charge into the computer. It had been a busy morning. After dropping Caden off at school, Susannah had been more than glad to get back into the groove of adjusting patients and writing notes. Since getting the phone call telling her that Angie was in jail, her life had been a nonstop whirlwind of caring for Caden, treating patients, and looking into Gus's murder. Discovering that Travis was still married and that his soon-to-be-ex-wife had met him at the campsite put a whole new spin on Angie's problem. A ride with Bitsy to Tussahaw Junction might provide some more information.

As if on cue, Bitsy entered the office, her concealed-carry handbag on her shoulder. "Hey, Miss Larraine." Sauntering up to the desk, she plopped her elbows on the counter. "Did you get all caught up on what we learned at America's Craziest gun store?"

"You mean finding out that Crystal was wearing boots that matched the footprints you two saw at the camp?" Larraine typed a few more strokes. "Good detective work. But I was

CHAPTER EIGHTEEN

shocked to hear about how Crystal acted."

"The porch light's on, but no one's home." Bitsy leaned in. "Do you think she could have done Travis in to get his share of the business?"

"I have no earthly idea what Crystal is capable of." Larraine pushed her bifocals up into her white hair. "I'm not sure we should be gossiping about someone who has mental health challenges."

"I think it might be more than that." Tina came in from the file room and handed Susannah a file. "I heard from my cousins who live in the Junction that Crystal might have substance abuse problems."

"I didn't know you had kin close by," Larraine commented.

"Miss Bitsy's not the only one with cousins scattered around the county. I used to spend a lot of time at their house." She smiled and tapped Bitsy's hand. "Remind me to tell you about the time I got lost in the old Civil War cemetery on Halloween."

"Oooh." Bitsy grinned. Even Larraine smiled. "Everyone has a least one good cemetery story."

"I don't," Susannah said.

"That's 'cause you're a Yankee. You all trudge down city sidewalks trick-or-treating for pizza slices." Bitsy pointed at Susannah. "Isn't that why New York City has an overpopulation of squirrels? They follow the kids around and steal pizza slices from their trick-or-treat bags. Didn't you tell me you once saw a squirrel riding a subway train with a slice of pizza in its paws?"

Tina burst out laughing. Susannah rolled her eyes. She didn't want to tell them it was a rat she had seen eating pizza on the subway.

Larraine logged off the computer. "I have some errands to

run." With a twinkle in her eyes, she retrieved her handbag. "You all have a good lunch and don't be late coming back."

"Bye, Miss Larraine." Tina turned to Bitsy. "Where are you two going?"

"To my cousin Shanice's print shop in Tussahaw Junction," Bitsy said. "I need some signs for Growl-A-Ween. Why don't you come along? I'll buy you lunch, and you can tell me your scary story."

"You two go ahead, I have to lock up." Susannah shelved her file and gave Rusty a quick belly rub before she climbed into the back seat of Bitsy's Ford Explorer. While Tina and Bitsy planned out their lunch, Susannah checked her phone. Angie's lawyer was working on a new bail hearing, and she didn't want to miss his message.

"Dr. Shine?"

Susannah stowed her phone. "Sorry?"

Tina gazed at her in the visor mirror. "I just asked how much you knew about the history of this part of the county."

"I remember reading up on Tussahaw Junction when I first moved here. The textile mill was built before the Civil War, wasn't it?"

"And so was the cemetery," Bitsy said, wiggling her hand in Tina's direction. "Booooooo."

"That's right." Tina twisted to see Susannah. "My uncle was a history buff, and he made us memorize all kinds of facts."

"Like what?"

"Well, the oldest homes in Tussahaw Junction were built by workers from the Tussahaw Textile Mill. Like Miss Bitsy said, both the mill and the cemetery have been here since the early 1800s. Everyone calls it the Civil War cemetery, but that's not completely correct. Some people even think it was built on an

CHAPTER EIGHTEEN

ancient Native American burial ground."

"I heard that they burnt witches at the stake there. That's why everyone's scared of it," Bitsy commented as they entered the outskirts of Tussahaw Junction. "It's full of antebellum ghosts and voodoo ghouls."

"No, I don't think—" Tina began.

Bitsy slowed as the traffic backed up for a red light.

Susannah asked, "Is that the cemetery you were talking about?" A large plot of land lay behind a low wrought iron fence. Weathered headstones were set away from the fence. Two figures huddled under a tree next to a large stone memorial. Susannah poked Bitsy. "And is that Travis Keene?"

Tina craned her neck to see past Bitsy. "Is that Crystal?"

"Where?" Bitsy stood on the brake.

"There." Susannah pointed. "Standing under that tree."

"I don't see anyone." Bitsy hung her head out the window. A car honked. "I hope it wasn't their ghostly doppelgangers. Seeing a doppelganger is hella bad luck."

After parking outside the print shop, Bitsy opened her glove box; she removed a small rabbit's foot and began rubbing it along the dashboard and around the steering wheel. She handed it to Susannah. "Here, you carry this for a while to ward off the bad juju."

"I'll stay here." Tina grinned as Susannah took the rabbit's foot.

Inside the shop, a clerk handed Bitsy a box of fliers. "Shanice had to leave, but these are for you."

"See, that bad juju is working against us already." Bitsy snatched the rabbit's foot from Susannah and rubbed it between her palms. "Shanice was supposed to dig up some dirt on Travis for us."

"Maybe there wasn't anything to dig."

Bitsy lifted one brow and pulled an orange sheaf of paper out of the box of fliers and waved it at Susannah. A color picture of a cocker spaniel wearing a jester's hat and flouncy collar danced before her. "At least these were printed before the change in juju. What do you think?"

"I think we have a winner," Susannah said. The cocker spaniel actually seemed to be enjoying the costume.

"Me too." Bitsy paused, eyeing a bulletin board. She peered at one of the ads, her brow scrunched. "What's this? A haunted house?"

Susannah grabbed the flier and tore it from the board. "No more haunted houses."

Bitsy wrestled the flier away from her. "That's tonight!" Bitsy spun, almost crashing into the clerk, who had returned with Bitsy's Growl-A-Ween signs. Susannah steadied the clerk. "I only have a few hours to get ready. Grab those signs." To the clerk, Bitsy said, "Tell Shanice I owe her." Clutching the box of fliers, she told Susannah, "Let's go!"

Susannah followed her out, jamming the yard signs into the open hatchback. Bitsy slammed it shut and jumped into the driver's seat. "Let's drive by this address." She handed the ad off to Tina. "I think it's on the other side of the cemetery. We can keep an eye out for Crazy Crystal and Two-Timing Travis."

"That's the old feed and seed store," Tina said. "You know, the one that backs up to the cemetery. My cousin told me the Tussahaw High seniors converted it into a haunted house to raise money for their senior prom."

"I love me a haunted house." Bitsy followed Tina's directions, and they soon saw the old building decorated for Halloween. "Dr. Shine, we have a date with destiny."

CHAPTER NINETEEN

Haunted House Holdup

Despite her best efforts, Susannah found herself in Bitsy's SUV dressed as Supergirl.

"Supergirl, for real?" Bitsy asked. "You're grown. Why not Wonder Woman?"

"I might be a wonderful woman," Susannah said as she tugged the Supergirl cape around her shoulders, "but I'm not going out in public in a teddy and a tiara. At least this outfit has sleeves. Besides, it's all I could find on short notice."

"It's Angie's, isn't it?"

"What if it is?" Susannah always felt foolish in costumes but admired Bitsy's ability to have fun dressing up. Her zombie makeup was impressive considering the small amount of time she'd had to get her look together. Even Andrea had commented on how quickly she had gotten dressed. "Anyway, remember what Andrea said. We need to be home early. We can't expect her to watch the boys for us all night. She has studying to do."

"We'll be back early. But let me get my Halloween classic rock groove on." Bitsy shimmied her shoulders to the beat of "Monster Mash." "You, know, I think a haunted house would make a good fundraiser for the Peach Grove Business Association."

"If you say so." Susannah smoothed her cape. "We'll need a passel of volunteers. But you're the president now, and you can probably motivate people better than Marcie could have."

"Oh." Bitsy stopped shimmying and turned the volume down. "I don't know about that. The only volunteer I motivated for Growl-A-Ween is you."

At the old feed and seed store, they parked in an empty lot that already was filling with cars. Keith Cawthorn sat in a Peach Grove PD cruiser, and Officer Chaffin directed traffic.

"Hey there, Officer Cawthorn." Bitsy waved at Keith as she and Susannah joined the ticket line. Ahead of them, Susannah saw Disney princesses and superheroes, but Bitsy's darker take on the costume was not unusual. There were several Ghostfaces in long black robes.

"Keep your eyes open," Susannah told Bitsy.

"For real-life ghosts and ghouls?" Bitsy stared into the cemetery. "We'll go looking for them later."

"No," Susannah whispered, "for Travis or Crystal."

"Why would Travis show up at a haunted house?" Bitsy frowned, gazing down the line. "Though I could see cray-cray Crystal dressing up as a serial killer."

Behind them, a teenaged Dracula swooped into line, swooshing his satin cape over his head and burying his fangs into the neck of a tall young woman who screeched with delight. Keith looked over and then exited his car.

"Look." Susannah pulled Bitsy's arm, pointing to a group of people coming around the corner of the building from the street. "Is that Travis?"

"Where?" Bitsy twisted, following Susannah's finger. "I don't see anybody. I think you're imagining things."

At last they paid their entrance fee and were ushered down into a damp cellar with about a dozen other people. A thin young man in ragged jeans and a black shirt pointed across the low-ceilinged room to a wooden staircase.

"Once you go up the stairs into the haunted house," he said as he looked from person to person, "you can't come back."

The group slowly treaded up the rickety stairs, Susannah and Bitsy the last to enter. Stepping onto an uneven floor, Susannah took a few small steps into the darkness, disoriented, feeling Bitsy's breath on her hair. A light suddenly flared, and a witch flew by on a broomstick. The flash of light and the sudden movement caused the women to jump, grabbing each other. Laughing, they continued on amid squeals of fright until their pace slowed and the temperature rose.

Bitsy touched Susannah's arm. "It's hot as the blazes in here. Let's see if we can get to the end—"

Before Bitsy could finish, Susannah was shoved. She crashed into the wall as her purse was yanked from her shoulder. At the same time, a yowling filled the air and a strobe light flashed. Large dead eyes flew at her. Bitsy ran away shrieking as a ghoul came at Susannah, its arms outstretched. She reached for her purse but became entangled in wires. The sound of tearing cloth and snapping plastic filled the air as the ghoul bobbed about her head.

"What's happening?" a voice yelled.

In her frenzy to get free, Susannah had twisted the ghoul's robes around her arms and face. She thrashed about, hitting several teens as they rushed past. The lights came up, and she blinked against the brightness.

"You broke it," a girl dressed as Harley Quinn accused,

pointing a baseball bat. Susannah flattened herself against the wall. "You ruined everything."

The same young man who had ushered them into the basement came down the hall with a walkie-talkie in hand. He took one look at the cracked plastic and ripped fabric and glared at her. "You're going to have to pay for that."

Susannah unwrapped the ghost's robes from her neck. "It wasn't my fault. Someone shoved me into the wall and grabbed my purse." She looked at the floor around her, her heart sinking. "I've been robbed."

"Well, someone has to pay, or I'm going to call the cops."

"Don't bother." Susannah untangled the last bits of string and fabric from her arms and plopped them into his hands in a jumble. "The police are outside. I'm going to make a report. One of your customers stole my purse."

Susannah gave Harley Quinn a hostile stare and stormed off. As she scanned the property for Keith or Owen, Susannah saw Bitsy entering the cemetery behind a black-robed ghost. A few steps ahead of them, a blue uniform hurried away.

"Keith?"

He didn't respond, instead disappearing behind the large hedgerow that grew over the fence between the haunted house and the cemetery. She pursued him, muttering. As she neared the fence, a high-pitched scream sent her running through the gate and into the dark cemetery.

CHAPTER TWENTY

Cemetery Smackdown

Illuminated by the orange glow of a streetlight, a narrow asphalt pathway wound between the tilted and weathered headstones. A group of costumed revelers gathered around a statue of a forlorn angel, and another shriek rent the air. High schoolers fooling around. Susannah stopped. Had she seen a police officer's blue uniform, or was it a costume? She heard voices and followed them, slowing her stride as the glow from the streetlight faded. Had Bitsy come this way too?

Another scream, followed instantly by a rolling boom.

Gunshot!

She crouched behind a monument, ears ringing. Low to the ground, she waited for another shot, but it never came.

"Hello?" she called. "Is there anyone there?"

"Susannah, is that you?" Bitsy answered from a distance. "Where are you at?"

"Over here." Susannah launched herself from a crouch, like a track-and-field athlete in pursuit of a medal, and then her foot hooked on something and she was eating grass. "Gah," she spit. *Cemetery grass.* She spit again. Her shoulder hurt and head ached. First slammed into a wall, now face-first into the ground. This was not her idea of a good time. Sitting up, she gasped as the image of what she had tripped on became clear. She crawled slowly toward a large granite tombstone.

"Don't be dead, don't be dead, don't be dead," she whispered to herself. But it was no use. On the other side of the headstone was the lifeless body of Travis Keene, a bullet hole in his forehead.

Frozen in place, she squeezed her eyes shut, tears flowing down her face. "Bitsy! Where are you?"

"Dr. Shine?"

She opened her eyes. Keith Cawthorn loomed over her. He put out his hand and helped her up. Bitsy appeared behind him, running down the path.

"I knew it! Zombies are real." Bitsy pushed past Keith and stared down at Travis with fear in her eyes. "Did you get bit?"

"Stop." Keith placed his large hand on Bitsy's shoulder, preventing her from going any further. "This is a crime scene now."

A few minutes later, Susannah, with a blanket over her shoulders, stood in the shadows where the blue light of Randy's patrol car flashed in the darkness. Shivering, she pulled the blanket tighter, covering up Angie's costume. She didn't know how she had torn the cape, or even how long she had been there; she just knew she was cold and tired. Randy stood over Travis, his hands on his hips, chewing on a toothpick. Detective Withers had taken Susannah's statement and was now interviewing Bitsy. The detective would return for a second round, Susannah was sure of it. Keith appeared holding two cups of steaming coffee in one massive hand and a flashlight in the other. He offered her a cup.

"Bitsy's going to take your nephew home and put him to bed.

CHAPTER TWENTY

And Tina wants you to text her if you need her in the morning."

"Thanks." Susannah warmed her hands on the cardboard cup. "And for the blanket."

"No problem." One of Keith's huge hands completely hid his coffee cup.

"How did you get here so fast?" Susannah looked up at him. "Before, I mean. After the gunshot."

"I was over there." He pointed over his shoulder, sweeping the beam from his high-powered flashlight around them in a widening arc. "The kids who run the haunted house reported that someone attacked one of their props and then ran off when they were asked to pay."

"That was me." Susannah sipped at her coffee, swallowing the lump in her throat with the brew. "Someone in the haunted house shoved me and stole my purse." She sighed. "I already told the detective. I couldn't pay, I didn't have any money. I came out looking for you." She stopped and shook her head. "I don't know what I saw."

"What do you mean?"

"I left the haunted house wanting to report the…" She searched for the right word. "The mugging. I came over here because I thought I saw you by the entrance to the cemetery." She shrugged. "I guess I was wrong."

Before Keith could say any more, the detective approached. He winked at Susannah and left.

"Miss Long didn't have much to add." Detective Withers pointed at Susannah with her pen. "She backs up your story of being shoved from behind. She said she got shoved too, and decided she had had enough and left. Is that correct?"

"Yes, but…" Susannah remembered the heat and the darkness. "I got shoved to the side. Into the wall, and I guess into the mechanisms that were running the ghost. Bitsy went forward." She looked at the detective. "There must have been two people working together."

"What makes you say that?"

"Because I was purposely pushed into the wall." Susannah rubbed her left shoulder. "The side opposite where I carry my purse. And then my purse was yanked off my arm. That same person couldn't have been rushing Bitsy and the others at the same time. It worked out for them that I got all tangled up and caused a scene. Nobody was paying attention to them when they left with my stuff."

"An interesting theory." The detective paused. "I told Ms. Long not to wait for you."

When the detective ushered Susannah past the front desk of the Peach Grove Police Department, Little Junior's brows rose so far up that it looked like he had two black caterpillars walking across his shaved brown head. As the detective ushered her into an interview room, she noticed Little Junior, head down, fingers moving furiously. The Peach Grove grapevine was smoking.

CHAPTER TWENTY-ONE

A 'Do and a Deer

Susannah walked into the kitchen, staring at her new phone. The smell of coffee and old sneakers hit her nostrils. She skirted Caden's gym shoes on the floor and sighed. After finding Travis Keene's body last night, Susannah was sure Angie would be released soon and she wouldn't have to lie to Caden anymore. He had asked about his mother on the drive to school this morning, and she had put him off. Hopefully, for the last time.

Susannah made a beeline for the espresso maker. It had taken an hour to replace her phone, but in the end she was satisfied with her choice. At least she had gotten to keep her old phone number. Once the service was turned on, the device began to beep and vibrate. Ten text messages from Bitsy appeared.

"No," she texted to Bitsy, "I really am not zombified." She added a winking emoji.

A phone message from an unknown number caught her eye. Since the voice mailbox hadn't been set up yet, she would not be able to retrieve the message. Sipping at her espresso, she peered at the instructions to activate the mailbox. As she swiped at the screen, the front door opened. Lunging across the table for her new concealed-carry purse, she withdrew her Glock, hands trembling.

"Suzie?" Angie grinned, one hand on Bitsy's arm. "I know you're angry at me, but can you drop the weapon?"

"Glad to see you using that handbag correctly, girlfriend." Bitsy removed the gun from Susannah's hand and placed it on the table. "Safety first."

"What? How?"

Angie rushed Susannah and engulfed her in a hug. "They released me!" Angie danced with glee. "My attorney showed up yesterday afternoon and told me about a new bail hearing this morning. They accepted all the paperwork you filed, and here I am. That squint-eyed detective was not happy, but there was nothing she could do. Anyway, by the time they let me use a phone, I couldn't get through to you."

"Enter *moi*." Bitsy crunched a Granny Smith apple as she closed the refrigerator. "I knew you were phone shopping, so I went."

"Thank you so much for helping me," Angie said.

Bitsy gave her shoulders a squeeze. "Don't mention it. Any family of Susannah's is family to me. Plus you're like the Italian grandma I never had. With all the best recipes I could ever want." She winked at Susannah. "I mean, I love her to death, but your sister thinks garlic-flavored flax crackers are a good substitute for Oreos."

"Thank you." Susannah hugged Bitsy.

"That's what friends are for. But I gotta fly." Bitsy twirled the apple and took another bite, crunching loudly as she headed for the door. "Don' forge yur air poinmet."

"What was that?" Susannah asked her sister.

"My hair." Angie dropped her bag. "I have to get cleaned up.

CHAPTER TWENTY-ONE

I have a hair appointment at Cutz & Curlz."

"What? Maggie's working? How did you even get an appointment?"

"I made an appointment before all this." Angie twirled her hand. "On the way over here, I got a call from Maggie's assistant, Polly. She'll be filling in for her." She raised her eyebrows at Susannah. Her expression said: *What do you think about that?* "I'm keeping the appointment."

"Well, let's get going." Susannah stowed her gun in the concealed carry purse. The one saving grace of last night's mugging was that she had not been carrying her Glock. She was now. Angie showered quickly and threw on a pair of jeans and a T-shirt. "I didn't know that you knew Maggie," Susannah commented as she pulled out of the drive.

"I don't," Angie replied. "Someone at work recommended her weeks ago, so I made an appointment."

When they entered Cutz & Curlz, a petite redhead bounded up to them. "Hi, I'm Polly Dean. I'm taking Maggie's clients today." Polly ushered them in and settled Angie into a chair. Susannah half expected to see Miss Shirleen under a dryer. Polly examined Angie's hair in the way only hairdressers do, half clinical tug and half loving caress. "I love these curls," Polly remarked. "Let's get you shampooed." To Susannah she said, "There's coffee in the break room. Help yourself."

"Thanks, I think I will." Susannah scuttled to the room where just a few days before, Maggie had asserted that Travis would be fine. Did Maggie feel guilty about assuming he was stepping out on her? Or would she be blaming Crystal for what had happened to him? Susannah had to admit that Crystal's part in this remained a mystery that needed solving. She glanced at the table, which was still covered with magazines and styling scissors. She looked around, searching for something that might jump out at her as being important, but nothing did. In the other room, Polly was busy shampooing Angie's hair. Susannah sprinted into action and opened the cupboards and even looked into the refrigerator, hoping something might scream, *I'm a clue!* But nothing did.

As she fixed herself a cup of coffee, a movement outside the building caught her eye. Like a lot of older Victorian-style homes, the window casing was framed out with thick wooden molding, and the bottom part was wide enough to sit on. She watched Otis, Maggie's mostly black cat, flick his tail and pick his way through some brambles. Susannah sympathized; any more coffee this morning and she would be twitching like a cat's tail. Otis moved further into the weeds and jumped atop something brown that was half hidden behind a small shed. Susannah squinted at it. It looked like the rump of a deer. The cat sat down and began grooming its paw. Susannah examined the brown thing more closely. Was it one of those fake deer bow-hunting targets?

Susannah made her way to the styling room where Polly was toweling Angie's hair. "Is that a deer hunting target in the backyard?"

"Mmm-hm." Polly nodded, a plastic rat-tail comb in her mouth. She removed it and used the long tapered end to spear through Angie's thick mane. "Travis left it here. Poor Travis." Her lip quivered.

Susannah immediately felt ashamed. "I'm so sorry." She hadn't meant to upset her. She had no idea that Polly even knew Travis.

"No, no." She waved the comb in Susannah's direction. "When I found out, you know, what happened." She took a

CHAPTER TWENTY-ONE

deep breath. "The first thing I thought about was the day he brought that dang deer over here. He was so proud of his new inventory that he just had to show it off to Maggie."

"Oh, that's so sweet," Susannah said, nodding and smiling at Polly, hoping she would dry her tears. In reality, it sounded odd and suspicious. Why would a man bring a hunting target to his girlfriend's hair salon? She envisioned caped women with their wet hair twisted into highlighting foils raising their hunting bows. She held back a laugh, biting the inside of her cheek. "Did Maggie hunt? Was it a gift?"

"Lord, no." Polly tittered. "Maggie hated anything outdoorsy. Her idea of camping out was tailgating in a parking lot before a Georgia game."

"I thought she went to the boys' camp-out," Angie said.

"Oh, sure." Polly grabbed a clip and clamped a section of wet hair. "She would do anything for her boys. But she wasn't like Travis. He loved all that stuff. He brought that thing over here just as proud as you could be and set it up against the toolshed. He shot at it with arrows and then left it here with all those arrows sticking out plain as day. Maggie lit into him about it, I can tell you."

"She did?"

"What do you think?" Polly blinked at her.

Susannah said nothing. She didn't know what she was supposed to think.

"Maggie wanted to have a fashionable, stylish atmosphere. Having a fake deer shot up in the backyard didn't exactly lend itself to our brand. It's ungainly."

Susannah said nothing. She was not an arbiter of what was fashionable or stylish.

"Men. Am I right?" Angie piped up. "I could tell you stories."

Polly winked at Angie, swiveled her in the chair, and began cutting. "I suppose I shouldn't say this about Travis, may he rest in peace, but he was a stinker about it."

"Tell me about it," Angie mumbled.

"He didn't want to take it back when Maggie asked him to. He insisted on leaving it in the yard. Maggie and I went out there and carried it behind the shed."

Susannah caught Angie's eye in the mirror. Her raised brow again asked Susannah, *What do you think about that?* This time, Susannah knew what she thought. Susannah winked at Angie. She thought she should get outside and dig around.

CHAPTER TWENTY-TWO

An Ungainly Ungulate

Susannah scurried out the door and ambled across the porch to the side of the building where the parking lot was. Trying for nonchalance, she tiptoed down the handicap-accessible ramp and strode through the backyard. A few trees speckled the area next to the parking lot, but the bulk of the yard was a rutted lawn and overgrown privet bushes. Past the bushes was a stand of trees that probably connected with the property behind her. The trees were so tall and numerous that anything else was hidden from view.

Susannah glanced at the house next door. The wraparound porch and railings were painted light pink, which contrasted nicely against the traditional gray of the house. A flash of movement caught her eye, and she saw a slat from a vinyl window blind drop into place. She shrugged. Was it trespassing if you were outside when you were supposed to be inside?

She secreted herself behind a dense thicket of overgrown privet, and then a sudden vibration frightened her so badly that she jumped. Lecturing herself on the adverse effects of too much caffeine, she pulled her phone from her pocket, palms sweating. This was why she disliked the sneaking-around part of being a snoop.

Her phone displayed a text from Bitsy: *Where are you?*

Texting with sweaty fingers took some time. After two failed attempts, she finally managed: *At Cutz & Curlz. Busy now, talk to you later.*

She didn't have time to explain to Bitsy that she was traipsing around Maggie Hibbard's overgrown yard because of her suspicion of a dupe deer. And at this point, she wasn't sure who exactly was the dupe.

Pocketing her phone, she paused to push a branch of privet out of the way. It slapped her arm, and she tottered into a ropy-looking vine with waxy, heart-shaped leaves. It was called *deer thorn* by her neighbors, and she recognized it too late. The innocent-looking dark green leaf hid a nefarious stem of miniature marauding thorns. The vine immediately lassoed her ankle as if it were alive. Grateful that she had donned a pair of walking shoes with thick soles, she shook her head. What was she doing here? She had designed the office schedule so that two mornings a week, no patients were seen. This was supposed to give her time to catch up on notes and reports, not sneak off into the hinterlands of someone's unkempt and bramble-ridden yard. She waggled her foot free and looked over her shoulder. The house next door was quiet, and she thought she heard a raucous laugh coming from Cutz & Curlz.

Angie was a people person, and Susannah wouldn't have been surprised to find out that she was delaying her haircut by keeping Polly in stitches with some stories of her pre-Caden party life in New York City. Susannah continued on, stepping around an anthill. In the distance, a freight train rumbled. Cutz & Curlz was close enough to the railroad tracks that the

CHAPTER TWENTY-TWO

train passing would cover up any noise she made examining the deer target—if she got there before it passed.

As the train neared, she felt its vibrations in the earth. Finally at the shed, she skittered behind it and examined the faux deer. Standing about four feet tall, the target was made of foam and taller than it looked from a distance, with a realistic-looking face and a ten-point rack. Susannah was surprised at what hunters would do to hone their craft. She patted its back and sides; it felt smooth and intact. Not many arrows had pierced the ersatz animal's hide. Why had Travis left it here? It was possible he wanted to show it off. But if so, why would he keep it here, half-hidden behind the shed?

As the locomotive reached the railroad crossing just yards from the salon's parking lot, it sounded its horn. The whistle was so loud, the noise would have covered the sound of a pack of wild warthogs making wild warthog love. Susannah quickly crouched down to get a better view of the target's side. Just behind the foreleg, where she supposed the vital organs would be found, was an oblong piece of foam that looked as though it could be removed. She bent lower and prodded it with her fingertips.

A tap on her shoulder sent the hair on her arms standing to attention. She twisted to see who was behind her and a pain shot up her spine. "Ow!"

"You okay?" Bitsy yelled over the sound of the horn, a look of concern on her face.

"Holy moly!" Susannah untwisted and rubbed her back. She shouted over the rumble of the train, "What are you doing here?"

Bitsy's words were obscured, but she pointed at the house with the pink porch. Susannah looked to see a woman in the window waving at them. *Cousins?* Susannah mouthed the word.

Bitsy gave her a thumbs-up.

What else is new? Susannah thought, pointing at the deer and mouthing the words, *help me*.

Bitsy wagged her finger at Susannah and then pointed down at Susannah's feet. "Back up."

Susannah scrunched her nose. *Back up?* She stepped back, eyes fixed on the legs of the target. Vines curled around them. She felt Bitsy tugging on her as the rumble of the train decreased. Bitsy leaned in and shouted: "You're standing in poison ivy!"

Susannah jumped back.

"That's better." Bitsy nudged her out of the way, lowering her voice as the train receded into the distance. "That's a Big Shooter Buck target. Little Junior had one."

"What's this?" Susannah asked pointing to the middle piece without getting close to the poison ivy.

"That there is a removable foam section." Bitsy pushed on it. "You can replace it when it gets all shot to smithereens."

"I want to see what this deer is hiding." Susannah poked it, and the piece shifted. She bent closer and then squeezed her finger inside the minuscule gap and tried to pull it loose. It didn't budge.

"I think we're going to have to lay this ungulate down," Bitsy said. "Then ram the piece out from the other side."

"Okay."

"Come on," Bitsy said, leaning over the target and pulling it toward her. "Its feet are all tangled up in these briars. Just tip it."

Susannah glanced at Cutz & Curlz and noticed Polly moving

around the break room. A shot of adrenaline spurred her on. They had to finish before the next client showed up and asked why two women were hiding behind her shed and molesting a make-believe buck. She grasped the animal around its middle and tipped it over. Bitsy shoved the foam section, and it came free. She held it up for them to see.

The piece was solid foam, but a cavity had been carved out in the middle. The hole was big enough to hide something about the size of a paperback book. The women locked eyes. Susannah shoved the piece back inside the target.

"Let's get out of here."

CHAPTER TWENTY-THREE

Pops & Cracks & Gangs

Susannah hugged her coffee mug in her hands and swiveled in her chair to look at Henry the Eighth. His bright tank made her smile. Henry swished his tail and circled his green moss ball. Susannah wished Caden was here to share this with her; his enthusiasm and excitement over a tiny fish and a bit of green moss was contagious. Placing her mug on her desk, she clicked her computer mouse and peered at the Google map from a different angle.

This morning, she and Bitsy had found themselves hip-deep—well, maybe ankle-deep—in brambles and vines, dissecting the foam guts from a faux deer. And what had they learned? She tapped a finger on the patient file Tina had given her and bit her lip. A modicum of Caden's enthusiasm could help her figure out how the secret hidey-hole fit into the overall picture. Though the connection between Gus and Travis was still tenuous, it was obvious to her that Travis had been involved in something underhanded. Using the inconspicuous foam target and hiding something in the cavity, Travis would have been able to communicate with another person without anyone ever seeing them together.

CHAPTER TWENTY-THREE

But why? The Google map of Peach Grove didn't provide any answers about Travis's motivation. Was he hiding something? Passing messages or money? She wanted to bring her discovery to Randy, but she remembered his admonition to her. Perhaps if she had proof of what the deer was used for, she could admit to Randy she had been snooping. Until then, it was her secret. Well, hers and her closest friends'.

The intercom buzzed.

"Dr. Shine?" Larraine's voice came through the speaker. "You have a patient in room two."

"On my way."

Angie had mentioned that Gus got phone calls and text messages that he ignored. He and Travis could have been communicating. But Susannah couldn't imagine any scenario where Gus would be traipsing around Maggie's yard without someone noticing. Bitsy's cousin Tiffany had seen Susannah as soon as she left the parking lot.

An idea tickled her brain, and she straightened her spine. If someone lived close by Maggie's shop, it might make sense. But the property behind Cutz & Curlz was owned by the city's water authority.

Susannah closed the map and gazed at the peach orchard across the street, now in hibernation. She stared at the naked branches and cleared her mind. Exhaling, she stood and with a small wave to Henry, walked down the hall. In room two, Mr. Doyle Etheridge was lying face down. She patted his shoulder. "Good to see you."

Doyle raised his head and gave her a wink before he buried his face in the papered head piece with a crinkle. Susannah palpated his back and pelvis while forcing all other thoughts out of her mind.

"Okay, let's get you onto your side." Susannah moved in for a pelvic adjustment. Doyle squinted up at her, his bushy gray eyebrows contracting. As she leaned into his pelvis, an audible *pop* filled the room.

"Just what the doctor ordered," Doyle wheezed, righting himself and sitting up. "I suppose you heard about the murder down in the Junction th' other night?"

"I did." At least it wasn't common knowledge that she had tripped over Travis's body.

"I heard some crazy rumors about that," Doyle commented. "You know, some people think there are spirits that walk the earth. Souls that refuse to stay in that cemetery." His raspy voice broke and his eyes narrowed to slits. "They walk the woods looking for souls to steal. If you look one in the eye, I've heard tell the sight is so horrible it just stops your heart." He paused, then cackled and broke into a grin. "You should see your face, Doc. Don't tell me you believe in all that hogwash?"

"Of course not." She winked at him. "For a moment, I thought *you* did."

"Me? I'm a man of reason," he said. "I got my rifle and I don't need no reason." He cackled again. "You see, Doc, I've lived down this end of the county all my life. I've hunted down yonder and roamed the woods around Peach Grove and Tussahaw Junction ten times over. If there were some demons out for revenge or evil spirits walking the earth, I would've met them by now. And I ain't. Unless you count the spirit inside some folk that just makes them mean."

He stood and reached for his keys and wallet, which he had left on a small shelf. "Ask me, it ain't the dead ones that give you a problem," he said, stuffing his wallet into his pocket. "It's the one's still walking."

CHAPTER TWENTY-THREE

"Can't argue with you there."

"Anyway, I heard from one o' my hunting buddies that a nine-millimeter kilt Travis. Never heard of no evil spirit that needed a gun."

Susannah stopped. A nine-millimeter bullet. She forced herself to focus on Doyle. "No, they wouldn't," she mumbled and ushered him toward the door. "I guess people are just caught up in Halloween."

"No, that's not it," Doyle said, jangling his keys and turning to her. "When I grew up, everybody I knew went huntin' in those woods. Got my first deer down the Junction out where that scout camp is now. Down there, used to be you could walk for miles and not see another soul. But there were certain areas everyone knew were off limits." He nodded at her and hitched up his pants, dragging out the story.

"Why?"

"Shiners."

"Shiners?" Susannah had a mental image of shoe shiners.

He grinned at the confused look on her face. "Moonshiners. Used to have a still down yonder. Everyone knew roundabouts where it was. Least, where to stay away from." The laugh lines on his face smoothed out, and for the first time he looked serious. "Nowadays, I don't know what goes on. I hear rumors. Drugs. Guns. Gangs. Don't usually believe what I hear, but with a man dead, I guess there's a good reason to keep away."

"I guess so," Susannah ushered him out of the treatment room. A plan began to form in her mind. Travis had last been seen in the cemetery, and tomorrow was his funeral. She understood his family had a plot in the same cemetery he had died in. Susannah shivered. Wandering around woods that went for miles would only get her lost, but a tromp around the cemetery would definitely be in order. She dashed to her office to make some calls.

CHAPTER TWENTY-FOUR

Zebra Bereaved

Susannah and Angie drove in silence to Tussahaw Junction and Travis's funeral. The area was just as small as Peach Grove, so it really wasn't surprising that the cemetery on the outskirts of town should house a lot of local residents. The real mystery was, why had Travis been in the cemetery in the first place? Was he hiding something there? Susannah glanced over to Angie, who had the vanity mirror down and was applying an extra layer of mascara.

"I don't know about you," Angie said, "but I'm not looking forward to this. Why'd ya force me to come? I didn't know Travis. The only time I ever talked to him was when he sold us our guns."

Susannah took a sip of her latte, inhaling the aroma. It had taken two shots of espresso to get her moving extra early this morning. She eyed Angie again. Her sister was chewing on a corn muffin, the crumbs sprinkled over her lap. "I didn't really know him either, but we need all hands on deck here."

"All hands on deck?" Angie laughed, a few more crumbs falling down her chin. "What are you, a sea captain? Did you used to talk like this in Brooklyn?"

"You know what I mean. Get off my back." Susannah looked down the road as she grasped the steering wheel. "At least I don't swear like a sailor and spit on the ground."

"I do not spit!" Angie turned to face her. "Except one time when Jimmy Massaro pinched me, and I never lived it down."

"I know. I know." Susannah felt a twinge of guilt bringing up the ancient accusation, but her sister deserved a jab once in a while. She teased Susannah often enough. "Let's go over what we have to do when we get to the cemetery."

Text messages had been coming in from Bitsy since the crack of dawn. Her new role as president of the Peach Grove Business Association had given her a new take on the situation. She had become point person, sending emails and text messages to the group and taking up a collection for a spray of flowers that had been sent directly to the funeral home. And while Susannah and Angie had begged off of going to the viewing at the funeral home, Bitsy had attended, ostensibly in her role as president, but unobtrusively as a spy for the Ladies' Crime-Solving Club, accompanied by her cousin Shanice. They had kept their eyes and ears open and had agreed on one thing: Crystal and Travis indeed were still married.

"I thought we were just supposed to snoop around," said Angie.

"Snoop, but with a little grace and decorum."

"Aye, aye, Captain," Angie mocked. "I'll see if I can find some decorum in my pocketbook."

"You know what I mean." Susannah tapped her sister's arm. "Don't make it obvious. No one is expecting us to be hanging over his coffin in despair. But we are in mourn—"

"Got it. I'll be appropriately bereft, but in a classy, understated kinda way."

CHAPTER TWENTY-FOUR

"At the cemetery, keep an eye out for anywhere Travis might have been hiding."

Susannah steered her Jeep into the parking lot of the First Methodist Church. Bitsy's SUV was already in the parking lot, and Susannah felt relieved that she would know someone in the church besides the deceased. Entering, she noticed Bitsy in a pew at the middle of the church, seated next to a woman who had to be Cousin Shanice. Bitsy's peach-colored fringed shawl highlighted her black, long-sleeved dress. She had a way of making her unorthodox clothing choices work.

As Susannah queued up to give her condolences, she locked eyes with Randy Laughton at the rear of the church and quickly looked away. At the front of the church, Crystal Keene stood next to an elderly couple and a middle-aged man who favored Travis. His parents and brother, perhaps? Crystal looked as hardboiled as ever, wearing a white blouse tucked into a dark pair of skinny jeans that clung to her thin legs. Her makeup was too heavy. Her lipstick, though light pink, somehow seemed a few shades too dark. She sported a pair of brown scuffed cowboy boots and her blond hair was piled on top of her head in an untidy bun.

"That girl needs a stylist," Angie whispered.

As they neared the altar, Susannah became aware of whispering. She turned to see Maggie Hibbard at the entryway, wearing a red dress. An audible hum began as more and more mourners twisted in their seats to look.

Bitsy left her pew and sidled up next to Susannah, whispering, "I thought the devil came in a blue dress."

Susannah bit her lip, but Angie let out a guffaw at Bitsy's reference to an old movie and an even older song. Maggie shot a look at them and then at the front of the church. Susannah swallowed, unable to look away as Maggie strode down the main aisle, her dress swishing in the now-silent church. Her high-heeled sandals, open-toed with black-and-white zebra stripes, clacked on the floor.

"Those're *safari night at the disco* shoes," Angie commented. Susannah discreetly swatted her.

Crystal leaned in and spoke to her in-laws, who stiffened. There was a collective sigh of relief as Maggie chose a pew about halfway back from the altar. Bitsy grinned. Maggie had chosen the pew right in front of Cousin Shanice.

Bitsy gave Susannah a nudge and whispered, "Gotta go." She tiptoed into the pew and swiftly settled in next to Shanice.

"Sorry, sis," Angie said *sotto voce* and quickly crossed the aisle and squeezed in next to Bitsy.

No sooner had Angie's backside hit the pew than Crystal, clearing her throat loudly, gripped her brother-in-law's arm and said, "I'll take care of this." She strode down the main aisle with an air of self-satisfaction. Stopping at Maggie's pew, she leaned her arm on the pew end and said, "You might should leave right now before things get ugly."

"I think they already *are* ugly," Maggie snarled at Crystal, taking her in from her stringy blond hair to her scuffed-up cowboy boots.

Crystal stepped back and gazed at Maggie. "Girl, you haven't got the sense that God gave you." A wan smile flitted across Crystal's face and then faded. Her smug expression returned. "Travis told me you were a loudmouth."

"And Travis told me you were a lush." Maggie wrinkled her nose and waved her hand in front of her face as if she smelled something unpleasant. "Which is why he left you and started seeing me."

CHAPTER TWENTY-FOUR

Crystal froze, her expression of triumph erased, her mouth and eyes rigid. Susannah noticed a twitch in her left eye.

"Now, get your nasty breath out of my face," Maggie finished, placing her black patent leather handbag on her lap and leaning back in the pew.

Crystal's face cracked. Grabbing Maggie's handbag, she yanked it out of her hands and threw it on the floor. "Travis loved me." She gritted her teeth and ground the patent leather under the heel of her boot, then poked Maggie's shoulder. "He was just using you. And when he was done with his business, he was going to leave you too." She hoisted her heel and stomped on the bag, scarring the leather, then nudged the toe of her boot under the handbag, lifting it.

Maggie stared in horror. "That's Kate Spade!"

"You"—Crystal glared at Maggie, her eyes slitted—"were just another one of his deals."

With a snap of her ankle, Crystal lifted Maggie's purse off the floor and launched it into the air. The scratched black projectile flew to the rear of the church, spewing its contents as it went. It landed with a slap. The church was silent for a moment, and then Crystal began to laugh, a long, low cackle.

"Fly away, little magpie." Crystal waved her hand at Maggie as she wheezed with laughter. The woman had obviously smoked one too many cigarettes.

"Travis was right!" Maggie jumped up, her eyes wide. She pointed at Crystal. "You're not just a drunk, you are deranged." With all eyes on her, she pushed past Crystal and fled down the aisle.

Maggie strode down the main aisle of the church, and Susannah met her at the last pew. Once Crystal had sent the bag airborne, Susannah had made her peace with not giving her condolences to Travis's family and bolted for the door. Bitsy and Angie sat stunned for a moment, then they too rose and followed the red-clad Maggie to the door.

Doyle Etheridge sat in the last pew next to Maggie's flattened purse. As she bent to pick up the remains of her bag, Doyle tilted his head and whispered to her, "Nice exit. Love them kicks." He wore a delighted smile and winked as he handed her a few personal items, including a tampon that had landed in his lap. Maggie didn't reply but stooped to pick up some makeup and her wallet.

Crab-walking into the next pew, Susannah retrieved Maggie's keys. Doyle twisted in his seat and in a stage whisper said, "Like I said, Doc, it's the live ones we have to worry about." Susannah patted his arm and followed Angie and Bitsy out the door and down the steps of the church, pursued by a few others, including the pastor.

Outside, Bitsy stood facing Maggie. "You all right?"

Maggie looked dazed.

"You certainly showed off your fashion superiority to them."

"Well, that wasn't my intention," Maggie said, then paused. "Or maybe it was. Not that it means much to that clan of troglodytes."

"Good one, Miss Maggie," Bitsy cooed at her. "You don't hear that kinda vocabulary every day."

Maggie raised one eyebrow at Bitsy. "Mostly I just wanted Crystal to see that I wasn't going to be cowed by her."

Susannah approached them. "Maybe we should get out of the way," she said as Crystal stuck her head out of the double doors, then pushed the doors open wide.

"You still here?" Crystal sneered at Maggie. "I'm fixin' to make you wish—"

CHAPTER TWENTY-FOUR

"Wish this." Maggie winged her handbag at Crystal like she was throwing a patent leather Frisbee. It flew true and hit Crystal in the head. She wobbled and slumped forward slightly, grasping the doors for support. Susannah moved into action, retrieving the purse, taking Angie under her arm, and then nudging Bitsy, who pushed Maggie from behind toward the parking lot.

"Step on it, girl, we gotta move," Bitsy said as Maggie burst into tears. "Now, don't go doing that. Travis is in a better place."

"I know!" she wailed, pushing her face into the shoulder of Bitsy's black funeral dress. She inhaled, heaving. "And I know he was still seeing that bleach-blond stringy-haired witch." Tears poured down her face. Bitsy took one arm, Susannah the other, and they propelled her through the parking lot.

"You can ride with me," Susannah said, and handed Maggie her purse. "I'll take you home."

Maggie straightened and then began to cry again. "I need a tissue."

Angie pulled a flattened tissue pack out of her bag and handed it to Maggie.

The black-suited pastor followed them into the parking lot and paused as Maggie honked loudly into first one tissue and then another. Susannah also noticed that Owen Chaffin had appeared on the steps but stayed put, viewing the circus from a distance.

Bitsy patted Maggie's back like she was a baby and said, "There, there."

The pastor approached, his face somber and his hands outstretched. "I'm very sorry, Miss. You have my condolences on your loss." He reached out to Maggie, but she backed away.

"I hope you don't take Mrs. Keene's actions as a reflection on the First Methodist as a church."

Susannah wondered if he had seen Maggie's retaliatory patent leather Frisbee fling. Was do-unto-others part of the First Methodist playbook?

Maggie wiped her nose with a balled-up tissue and straightened her spine. Susannah could almost see her thoughts, and they weren't ones of peace, love, and reconciliation. Even her stripy-strappy sandals seemed straighter. "I suspected Travis wasn't being honest with me, but I took my chances believing that he was a good man." She pulled a clean tissue from the pack, looking up at the man with eyes that now matched her dress. "But if he was married to that mess"—she tilted her head toward the church to indicate Crystal—"then that's all the proof I need that he was demented himself."

The pastor looked away, then back. "Just as long as you don't hold it against us none. Everyone grieves differently, Miss."

Maggie waved her purse in front of the pastor's face. "'Grieves differently'? I came here to pay my respects to a man I thought I was going to marry. And that lunatic smashes up a $250 handbag." She ignored the man and spoke to the women. "I just want to find my keys and go home. Has anyone seen them?"

The pastor shrugged and walked away. Susannah handed Maggie her keys along with a pen and another tampon. Maggie took the keys and stared at the feminine protection, then said, "Why did I get involved with him?" Instead of more tears, Maggie stamped her foot and spluttered. "And why did I have to get my period this morning? It wouldn't have been so bad if my Tampax hadn't been flying around consecrated spaces."

Bitsy leaned in and patted her arm. "I know," she said in her most soothing tone. "My first day is always the heaviest too."

With that, Maggie giggled, and the women all joined in until Susannah had tears in her eyes. "Let's get you home. I can take you if you don't want to drive."

"I can drive myself," Maggie said, raising her keys. "Thanks for the offer."

Susannah and Angie headed toward the Jeep. Maggie opened her car door and threw the purse on the passenger seat.

Bitsy nudged Susannah. "Here comes Crystal, and she looks mad."

The women exchanged glances. Susannah helped Maggie into her car and shut the door. On the steps of the church, Crystal waved Randy away and teetered into the parking lot. Bitsy sprinted to her SUV, jumping in and mashing the door lock button.

As Crystal neared, a weird, lopsided grimace on her face, a horn sounded. Angie was in the driver's seat of Susannah's Jeep. The engine came to life, and she maneuvered the vehicle between Crystal and Susannah.

"Get in!" Angie yelled at Susannah, who hopped into the passenger seat and pulled the door shut faster than she would have thought possible. Apparently, extra caffeine came in handy in funeral emergencies. Angie peeled out of the parking lot and into the street without a backward look.

In the mirror, Susannah watched as Crystal leaned on the hearse, rubbing her forehead.

Angie grinned. "I think I'm getting used to Southern life."

CHAPTER TWENTY-FIVE

Sherlock Hound

Susannah glanced over at her sister and laughed. "I've never seen a funeral like that before."

"*Madonna!* You and me both." Angie laughed. "I thought my friends at the bowling alley were wild. These people weren't even drinking!"

"Well, we don't know that for sure."

"That Crystal is a real *gavone*. She was out for blood. And Maggie, that girl is a hoot! Who goes to a funeral in a red dress and four-inch heels?"

"I guess a jilted hairdresser does," Susannah replied.

"What now, Captain? Do you have a plan B?"

Susannah had pulled her phone from her thankfully intact purse. About to call Bitsy, she paused midtap. "Plan B?"

"Yeah, ya know. We were supposed to follow the funeral procession to the cemetery. Right?"

"Yeesssss." Susannah stretched out the word. "We were."

"Well, should we go there now? Or come back for some post-funeral snooping?"

Quickly looking over her shoulder, Susannah made sure Crystal wasn't following them. She had the feeling that

CHAPTER TWENTY-FIVE

someone was staring at her, boring a hole into the back of her head with their eyes. But no one was there. It was just Catholic guilt.

"Let's go now." A few more taps, and Bitsy picked up. "Hey, we're doing a pre-funeral snoop of the cemetery."

"Aye, aye, Captain," Bitsy said.

Susannah shot a look at Angie.

"I think we'll need all hands on deck." Susannah heard Bitsy chuckling as she hung up.

Angie pulled into the cemetery, driving through a wrought iron gate set into stone pillars. Susannah remembered Travis's unseeing eyes and shuddered. They passed a towering oak, and acorns popped under the Jeep's tires as they wound their way around the paths.

"This looks like the place." Susannah pointed. "That's where I saw Travis before he was shot."

"Don't ya mean his doppelganger?" Angie chuckled as she put the Jeep into park. They got out, and Susannah walked toward the tree, sure now that it had been him and no doppelganger. The area was newer and better kept than where she had found his body. Here, there was nothing to see and nowhere to hide.

"What's this?" Angie poked something with the toe of her shoe.

A cigarette butt lay flattened in the road. Susannah bent to examine it. "A Marlboro." She leaned into the Jeep and pulled her phone out of her purse and took a photo. "Only the most popular brand of cigarettes in the country."

"Also Crystal's brand. And look." Pointing at the tip of the filter, Angie squinted. "There's lipstick on it."

Crystal's shade of pink. Picking up the butt with her fingernails, Susannah put it in her pocket.

"Ew, Suzie."

"Let's go." Susannah climbed into the passenger seat. "There's nothing else here. Follow this road. I think it will take us into the older section by the haunted house."

"You were right." Guiding the car around the asphalt road, Angie murmured, "Travis and Crystal were here. But I'm not sure how that's going to help us now. Unless, maybe Crystal did kill Travis."

"A cigarette butt isn't going to prove that."

Angie nodded and tapped the brakes. There was no mistaking where Travis had been found. Crime scene tape flapped in the breeze. They got out, and Angie came around the car and grabbed Susannah's hand and they walked across the grass and past several headstones.

"I'm sorry you have to keep tripping over dead guys." Angie squeezed her hand. "But I don't know what we're gonna find that the crime scene techs didn't."

"I've been thinking the same thing." They stood silently for a moment. Susannah turned as the sound of a dog's angry barking came down the road. She squeezed Angie's hand. "Let's get out of here."

Her sister reached into her shoulder bag. "I think I have some hair spray in here." She looked up at Susannah. "You know, in case a dog attacks."

A canine squeal rang out, and both women jumped.

"Is it a feral dog?" Angie stepped back.

The growls and yip-yaps neared. Susannah checked out the distance to the Jeep. An obelisk monument with a wide, stair-stepped base stood between it and them. "Maybe we should go this way."

"Good idea," Removing a trial-sized can of Aqua Net from

CHAPTER TWENTY-FIVE

her bag, Angie took the top off and shook it frantically. Beside her, Susannah crept behind the base of the monument. "If it attacks, I'll be ready."

As the sound came closer, they crouched. Angie held the mini-Aqua Net out in front of her, hand much steadier than Susannah's would have been.

"Yoo-hoo!"

At Bitsy's call, Susannah stiffened. Hadn't Bitsy heard the barking? "Over here." Trying to keep her voice low, she sounded hoarse. Bitsy came into view, her phone out, tapping on the screen. With Angie at her side and still aiming, Susannah stepped out from behind the memorial.

"What are you all doing?" Bitsy lowered her phone as she tiptoed into the grass. Her heels were almost as high as Maggie's. "Did you find something back there?"

"*Madonna*," Angie berated. "Get over here. Don't you hear that wild dog?"

Hand on her hip, Bitsy shook her head. "Are you funnin' me? Is this some kind of Yankee Halloween prank?"

Moving to Bitsy's side, Susannah listened. The barking was close now, but the closer the sound came, the more she realized it was not that of a wild dog. It sounded more like a painful yapping than a ferocious growl. She tugged at Angie's sleeve and motioned toward the path behind Bitsy with her chin. "I don't think you're going to need that."

A forlorn-looking Basset hound wearing a cape and a hat padded into view. He gave a few more yaps and a growl as he twisted around, chewing and snapping at the costume. Angie chuckled and called the dog. "Aw, sweetie, come here." She pronounced *come here* as her *com-ear*, but the dog seemed to understand Brooklynese and trotted over. "Are you stuck in that bad costume? I probably have some nail scissors in here." Angie looked into her bag. "We can cut it off."

Spreading her arms wide, Bitsy stooped down and shielded the dog. "You're not ruinin' Apollo's costume."

"Apollo?" Susannah asked. "How do you know his name is Apollo?"

"Because I helped name him." Bitsy gave the hound a squeeze, and he panted. "This here specimen of canine excellence is going to lead us to some clues, while at the same time showing off his insanely cute Sherlock Holmes costume. It's a couples costume, you know. And I have a matching cape and cap."

"He doesn't seem to like it," Angie pointed out.

"Nonsense." The dog drooled as Bitsy patted him. "He has a slight issue with stress-induced psoriasis. I gave him his medicine right before we left the house. He should be right as rain in a few minutes. Anyway, it's actually better his skin is covered up. That's the only way my cousin Kiara would let me take his cone off."

Susannah nudged Angie and mouthed *don't ask*. To Bitsy, she said, "Okay, tell Apollo to lead on."

"That's not how it works. We have to give him something to scent on."

"Like what?"

"I don't know." Scanning the surrounding area, Bitsy's shoulders drooped. "Kiara trains him with an item of clothing."

"What a cutie. I love animals." Slinging her shoulder bag across her body, Angie crouched and patted Apollo. "Um, Travis's funeral is gonna be here soon. Whichever way this is gonna work, let's get it going."

"I think this is a bad idea," Susannah said, crossing her arms. "We don't have anything for him to scent on, and Angie and I

CHAPTER TWENTY-FIVE

have looked around. There's nothing here to find. I think we should just leave."

Bitsy pouted. "Just give him five minutes."

"Okay, five minutes."

They looked down. Apollo was gone.

CHAPTER TWENTY-SIX

Bassett Fun Run

Apollo had made it four rows away and was watering a Civil War–era marker, his deerstalker cap tilted slightly.

"No, no." Angie's hands flew to her face. Hissing as she ran, she signaled to Susannah to follow. "Help me! We can't let him whiz on a grave. It's disrespectful."

The Basset hound ignored her, finished his business, and loped away.

"See?" Bitsy joined Angie in pursuit of the Basset. "He's feeling better already."

Treading between headstones, Susannah followed the women. If a dog relieving his bladder on the stone was disrespectful, what would three women tromping right over the graves be? At least they would get marks for dressing appropriately.

"Apollo, sweetie." Bitsy made kissy noises. Apollo twisted to face her, his sad brown eyes flicking up.

Susannah stopped, surprised at how well trained the dog was, but then he gnawed at his costume a few times and took off.

CHAPTER TWENTY-SIX

"He's not trained to voice commands yet."

Apollo climbed an embankment, sniffing the roots of a large oak tree. Beyond it, Susannah noticed an open grave and a man in a black overcoat setting up chairs. "No."

Angie followed her gaze, her eyes wide. "He probably smells the soil."

Already at the bottom of the oak, Bitsy found her progress slowed by her high heels. The absurdity of the situation struck Susannah. Bitsy in a black dress was a stark contrast against the dying grass and light-colored headstones. Apollo, cape still in place, wagged his tail and headed for the chairs. Apparently his meds had kicked in, and his short, powerful legs carried him along faster than Bitsy could keep up with.

"Did you see that?" Angie tilted her head.

"No, what?"

"That man, on the sidewalk over there." She pointed in the same direction Susannah had just been gazing. "He was wearing one of those Ghostface masks. I thought he was staring at me." She shuddered. "Those masks give me the creeps."

"Me too." Susannah stopped. "Ghostface?"

"Yeah, you know." Angie's shoe came loose and she stopped, throwing a twig to the side and fixing her footwear. She looked up, scowling, as if to lecture the oak tree for making life difficult, then turned her gaze to Susannah. "From the movie *Scream*."

"I know. I've seen a few of them already this year," Susannah said. "I'm starting to think it's not just a coincidence."

"What do you mean?"

"I..." Susannah took a breath. It must be her imagination. Where had she seen the Ghostface mask before today? Before she could collect her thoughts, there was a yell from over the embankment. "Maybe one of us should go get the car."

"I'll go." Angie scrambled out of sight.

Susannah followed the howling. Holding her shoes out, Bitsy appeared from behind a tree. "I knew Apollo was part bloodhound!" she exclaimed. "He found a gun!"

"What?" In all her pre-snoop preparation, Susannah had not envisioned finding a gun. "Where?"

"I already called the police." Bitsy waved her phone from side to side.

Susannah was stupefied. As she charged up the grassy knoll, her heel snagged an oak root. She tried to right herself and Bitsy reached out, but she fell, tumbling down the gnarly roots of the tree and landing at the base of a tombstone. Opening her eyes, she found herself face-to-face with an automatic handgun and Apollo's watery tongue. Apollo huffed loudly, drizzling her with drool, got to his feet, and snatched the pistol in his droopy jaws. Before Susannah could right herself, he trotted off.

"Take my hand." Bitsy's voice quavered, her hand with the high heels shaking. "He's headed for Travis's grave. Come on!"

Susannah stood, tugging her skirt down and brushing off a clod of dirt and some dead leaves. Taking off her shoes, she dashed after Bitsy. The man in the overcoat looked up as Apollo sped past the chairs and stopped at the edge of the grave, sniffing. The Basset dropped the gun into the grave, headed into the pile of excavated soil, and began slewing it into the open hole.

Fifteen minutes later, Randy was standing with his hands on his gun belt, peering down into the grave. An officer wearing purple latex gloves handed the gun up. Randy gripped the

CHAPTER TWENTY-SIX

weapon by the stock with two gloved fingers and removed the magazine. Scowling at Susannah, he placed the gun inside a cardboard container and then beckoned her to follow. At the tombstone where Apollo had originally found the gun, he pointed at Bitsy, who leaned against the tombstone while wiggling her toes. "Stay right there."

The tombstone was cool as Susannah leaned next to Bitsy and gazed around the cemetery. Past the open grave, the cemetery road looped and ended in a cul-de-sac at the wrought iron fence. A line of limousines and mourners' vehicles waited for Randy to release the site and allow Travis's interment to proceed. The dark-tinted window of the lead limousine rolled down, and Crystal glared at them. Susannah felt her face get hot as Crystal continued her South Georgia evil eye jinx. Officer Chaffin, who had been directing the cars and limos, approached the limo's window and inclined his head as he spoke to her. The curse was broken.

"Dr. Shine." Randy's gruff voice startled her. "Let's go over this again. This time slower. Why were you here before the funeral?"

At a loss for words, Susannah felt a drop of sweat trickle from her hairline down her neck. Randy had been at the church and had seen the ruckus with Crystal. Normally her inability to tell convincing lies made these kinds of situations stressful, but a brilliant fib came to her. "Well, given what happened at the church, we decided to come here and wait to pay our respects."

"Uh-huh," Randy commented. "And what does your sister have to do with this sudden discovery of a firearm?"

"Nothing." Susannah swallowed. A second trickle of sweat followed the first one. "She was in the Jeep the whole time. She doesn't even know Travis. She just came to keep me company."

Randy turned on Bitsy. "And that's your story too?"

"Angie was in the Jeep the whole time," Bitsy agreed.

"Are you sure about that?" Randy turned and pointed at Apollo, who had fallen asleep, his Sherlock Holmes deerstalker hat tipped down over one eye. "I thought you made a detour to get the Hound of the Baskervilles."

"Just for a minute," said Bitsy. Apollo growled in his sleep, his legs moving as if he were running, and she nudged him with her bare foot. "And I might add, this here dog is a purebred Basset hound." Bitsy jutted her chin at Randy.

Susannah made a signal with her hand, telling Bitsy to cut it short, but she didn't see it. Or if she did, she ignored it.

"He probably just solved your murder case," continued Bitsy.

"Hot dog." Randy raised an eyebrow at Bitsy, who put her hand on her hip. They had known each other since high school, and Susannah understood why they weren't friends. "Let's not get excited about this discovery too soon. Our ballistics team will tell us all about it. Until then, all we know is that we found a pistol."

"Hmmpf." Bitsy folded her arms, her shoes swinging.

Randy glared at Apollo, his jaw working as if he were pondering a way to arrest the animal. He shifted his gaze to Susannah. "Let me make one thing abundantly clear. If we find so much as a smudge on that gun that points to Angela Rossi, I will personally be knocking on your door to arrest your sister." Bitsy gasped, and Randy glowered at her. "And you better steer clear of this investigation too. Do I make myself clear?"

"Aye, aye," Bitsy mumbled.

"Now get away from my crime scene and take Mr. Holmes with you."

CHAPTER TWENTY-SEVEN

Frittata For Five

Spearing a potato with the tip of her fork, Susannah went tine-to-tine with Bitsy to finish the remnants of Angie's Italian sausage, egg, and potato frittata, always a family favorite. Angie had offered to cook after texting Tina and Larraine to update them on the happenings in the cemetery. They had both jumped at the chance for a late breakfast with Angie at the stove. Naturally, Bitsy had detoured to Susannah's house with Apollo in tow. Divested of his cape and deerstalker, Apollo lay on the living room carpet, face on his paws, snoring.

"That was delicious," Larraine said. "I've never had an omelet served on Italian bread before."

"Me either." Clenching a small piece of Italian bread, Tina raised it like she was toasting Angie. "I love the flavors, sausage and garlic and onions with some potato thrown in. Kinda like an Italian version of a Jimmy Dean's sausage-and-egg breakfast sandwich."

"You said it," Bitsy chimed in. "You should have tried it with the cheese and pasta sauce on top. It's kinda like a messy pizza-omelet." She quirked an eyebrow at Angie, who was giving her a playful frown. "Messy in a good way, like meatball hero kinda messy. Ooey-gooey goodness."

"Okay." Larraine aimed her thumb at Tina. "We need to hear more about what all happened this morning. Maggie got into an argument with Crystal—"

"It was more like a violent game of Frisbee using a Kate Spade handbag," Bitsy pointed out.

"What's that supposed to mean?" Tina's brown eyes gleamed as she popped the bread into her mouth.

Using her fork for emphasis, Susannah described the confrontation between Crystal and Maggie, punctuating with a stabbing motion the part where Crystal stomped on Maggie's bag.

Larraine crossed her arms, her thin fingers playing with the sleeves of her white cardigan. "That's very disrespectful."

"*Madonna mia!*" Angie said, pressing her middle and index fingers into her thumb and shaking her hand. "You shoulda seen the two of them. Maggie really provoked Crystal, coming into church all trussed up like a *puttana* in that dress and those shoes. She's my hero."

"Mine too," Bitsy said. "She must have superhuman wrist strength from doing all those comb-outs. She slung that handbag like an Olympic boomerang athlete."

"Okay, okay," Tina giggled. "First, there's no such thing as an Olympic boomerang athlete."

"Well, there should be."

"Second," Tina continued, "I think you need to start at the beginning."

"Right," Larraine said, "and don't leave out the part about the gin you found in the cemetery. I don't understand that part."

"Gin?" Bitsy narrowed her eyes. "We didn't have no gin in the cemetery."

CHAPTER TWENTY-SEVEN

Tina and Larraine looked at each other. Retrieving her phone from her bag, Tina pointed at the screen. "Right here, *Apollo found gin by tombstone.*"

Angie chuckled. "Autocorrect. I meant gun."

"Gun?" Larraine and Tina said simultaneously.

"Okay, ladies." Larraine sat back. "From the top. Slow."

The espresso machine gurgled while Angie and Bitsy recapped, from Maggie's flying feminine protection to Crystal's cranium getting creased. Bitsy added her quick detour to Cousin Kiara's to pick up Apollo and his psoriasis medication, leaving the bit about him sniffing out the gun for last.

Tina beamed. "I think Apollo broke the case."

"Could be." Angie placed a plate of cookies on the table. "What do you think Crystal meant by what she said to Maggie?"

"What did she say?" Larraine asked.

"That Travis was using her," said Susannah. Warming her hands around her demitasse cup, she frowned.

"That's terrible," Tina said. There were murmurs of agreement, and Tina tapped a nail on the table. "I've heard Crystal could be cruel, but what did she mean about his *business*? Not…" She shot a glance to Larraine, and her voice trailed off to a whisper. "Sex?"

Larraine, holding a butter cookie topped with sprinkles, froze.

"I've been thinking on that," Bitsy said, "and I imagine it has something to do with that hidey-hole me and Susannah found."

"I think so too," Susannah agreed. "But I can't figure out what kind of business she meant. Although I have been going over something Doyle Etheridge said the other day."

"What did he say, Dr. Shine?" asked Tina.

"He told me that he grew up down in the Junction and has

been hunting in the woods down there his whole life."

"Boring," Angie said. "Is that all?"

Throwing a dish towel at her sister, Susannah half huffed, half snorted. Angie giggled, but Susannah ignored her. "He said that there are rumors of criminals using the woods down in Tussahaw Junction to hide their activities. Years ago, it was moonshiners, but now he's heard about drugs and guns."

"Could Travis have been mixed up in something like that?" Tina asked.

"Little Junior did mention those meetings with the county task forces." Bitsy sat up. "They deal with guns and drugs."

"And Maggie told us that Travis was always traipsing around the woods," Susannah said. "Maybe he was running with some gang."

"Well, that would make some kind of sense then." Larraine's eyes became unfocused as she thought.

"I mentioned that hidey-hole to Keith," Tina said. "He actually got kind of grumpy about it and told me I should mind my own business."

"Really?" Susannah blurted before she could stop herself. "That's not like Keith."

"I know." Shaking her head, Tina twisted her wedding ring. "He seems to have something on his mind lately."

"How does all this tie into Gus's murder?" Larraine asked.

"I've been thinking about that," Angie said. "Remember I told you that Gus offered to change the sights on my Glock? Well, I didn't ask him to do that." She kneaded the towel in her fingers. "The more I think about it, the more I get the feeling that he was too interested in that gun."

"How do you mean?" Susannah asked.

"Well, it was always Gus who was bringing up the gun and

CHAPTER TWENTY-SEVEN

shooting. He told me he wanted to take me to the range. I remember when I told him that I shot with youse." Angie paused, laughing as her sister cringed at the Brooklynism. "He got a little annoyed. He really wanted me to go to Travis's to train."

Up until recently, the women had trained together monthly at a county-run range. Susannah had been very impressed by the rigorous safety standards there and didn't want to use the small range Travis had opened in America's Finest.

"Why would he get annoyed?" Larraine asked

"I'm not sure," Angie answered slowly, closing her eyes briefly as she collected her thoughts. "At first, I thought maybe he was trying to make a date of it, and I stepped on his plans."

"Oooh, a date at the range." Bitsy rubbed her palms together. "Like one of them zany Marx Brothers movies. You know, *A Night at the Opera, A Day at the Range.*"

"*A Day at the Races,*" Larraine said softly, nibbling on the cookie.

"Say what?" Bitsy asked.

"*A Day at the Races,*" Susannah said loudly. "The movie is called *A Day at the Races*, not *A Day at the Range*. Not that it matters."

"No, it might not," Bitsy agreed, "but it just occurs to me that someone else is super interested in guns."

"Who?"

"Crystal." Picking up a small wedge of toasted corn muffin lying on her plate, Bitsy popped it into her mouth. "Remember what she was doing that day at America's Finest?"

"How could I forget?"

"What do you mean?" Tina glanced from Bitsy to Susannah.

"Crystal was quizzing me about my gun. I thought she was

about to pat me down."

"Or do a strip search," Bitsy added

Susannah thought about it. "Well, Crystal is a bit odd."

Bitsy chortled, "That girl is a few fries short of a Happy Meal."

Tina covered her mouth; cookie crumbs spilled out from behind her hand.

"Think about it, Suzie," Angie said. "There's something weird about it, is all. I bet you could fit a gun in that deer."

Tina's phone rang, and she glanced at it. "That's Keith." She looked at Larraine. "He finally returned my call."

"Go on then," Larraine told Tina as she stood and took a few dishes to the sink. "Keith was gone when Tina got up this morning. She's been trying to track him down all day."

Purse on her lap, Bitsy pulled her Smith & Wesson from its holster and weighed it in her hand.

"What are you doing?" Susannah asked.

"Is that loaded?" Larraine raised her eyebrows.

"Uh, not anymore." Hitting the magazine release, Bitsy pulled back the slide. "I reckon this could fit in that hidey-hole."

"I bet mine could too," said Susannah. Glancing into the living room, she located her purse. As she picked up her bag, she noticed Tina staring at her phone. "Are you okay?"

"No." Tears streaked her face. "Keith's been arrested."

CHAPTER TWENTY-EIGHT

Off-Duty Debacle

Susannah embraced Tina as Larraine rushed over, wrapping her arms around both of them. "Tell me what happened."

"I didn't want to say because I couldn't believe anything was wrong." Tina inhaled, hiccupping, as Angie and Bitsy also came to her side, Susannah relaxed her embrace and Bitsy took her place.

"Give the girl some air." Larraine shooed them all away. "Go on, sugar."

Angie handed her a box of tissue, and Tina sat on the couch and blew her nose. "Right before you came to pick me up, Detective Withers stopped by the house. I don't like her, you know?" Tina paused. They all knew what she meant. Detective Withers had questioned her and Keith several times over the summer, trying to pin a murder on Susannah. "Keith went out to talk to her, and he didn't come back in."

"Where is he now?" Susannah asked.

"He's at the Peach Grove Police Department," Tina said, tears coming again. "They're holding him for questioning."

"For what?" Susannah said, her voice a little higher than she intended.

"He wouldn't say."

"If that Detective Withers is involved," Bitsy jumped in, "then you know she's probably barking up the wrong tree."

At the word *barking*, Apollo lifted his head.

"I've been telling myself that," Tina said, wiping the tears off her cheeks with the back of her hand as she gave Bitsy a weak smile. "That's what worries me. Keith's been acting a little weird since our Halloween party. I've asked him a few times to tell me what's wrong, but he keeps telling me it's nothing."

At a loss for words, Susannah glanced at Bitsy, who was tapping on her phone—contacting Little Junior, she hoped. Keith was a gentle giant and had always been somewhat transparent, for a cop. There was no way Susannah could imagine him doing anything that would negatively affect his family.

"Oh, darlin'." Larraine lowered herself onto the couch next to Tina and patted her thigh. "It's gonna be okay. It must be a mix-up of some kind."

Tina leaned into Larraine, and Susannah could not help but fixate on her pregnant belly. It had to be a mistake. With a baby on the way, it just wasn't possible that he would do anything wrong.

"It might be a mistake." Tina looked at Larraine. "But he asked me to get him a lawyer."

A few minutes later, Tina left, supported by Larraine, who promised to get her in to see her attorney, Winston Norris. Over the summer, Larraine had offered the same assistance to Susannah, but she had stubbornly refused the help. Today, Susannah thought Tina should take it. Susannah closed the door and ran back to where Bitsy and Angie were at the kitchen

CHAPTER TWENTY-EIGHT

table, heads together, looking at Bitsy's phone.

Elbows on the table, Angie was kneeling on her chair and peering at Bitsy's phone. She glanced up. "Little Junior's on it."

Susannah chuckled, noticing a similarity between her sister and her best friend. That was a phrase she had heard Bitsy use many times. "What did he say?"

"He said that Randy and Detective Withers have been in closed-door meetings all week." Bitsy's phone vibrated again.

"He said that when they brought Keith in, it looked friendly," Angie filled in while Bitsy read. "It wasn't until Little Junior went on his coffee break that he saw them fingerprinting Keith."

"Fingerprinting?" Susannah swallowed. She sank into the chair next to Angie and found herself stroking her sister's hair. Angie leaned in and gave Susannah a hug. Did this mean that her sister was no longer a suspect in Gus Arnold's murder? "Does this have to do with Gus or Travis?"

Bitsy put the phone down and tapped a long orange nail on the table. It made a sharp sound. *Click, click, click.* She looked from Angie to Susannah. Susannah felt her stomach sink. It wasn't like Bitsy to be at a loss for words.

"This is all my fault," Bitsy mumbled, her nail clicking a slow rhythm. "I really didn't think that Apollo was a superhero search dog. I just took him because I wanted the matching costumes. That deerstalker hat is dope."

"What is she talking about?" Angie whispered to Susannah.

"I don't know."

"You know I can hear you." Bitsy looked up, her huge brown eyes filled with tears. The clicking stopped. "The gun we found at the cemetery belongs to Keith. It's his off-duty weapon. A nine-millimeter Glock."

Stunned, Susannah said nothing. Angie slid down into a sitting position.

"Randy identified it at the scene because of the serial number." Bitsy curled her hand around her coffee mug and brought it into her chest, her thumbs stroking the ceramic. "They already sent it to the ballistics lab, and they're arresting Keith for both murders."

CHAPTER TWENTY-NINE

Evasive Evidence

Susannah gave Bitsy a squeeze. "This is not your fault."

"I can't believe it." Pacing back and forth across the kitchen, Angie grabbed a sponge and began scrubbing the stove. As quickly as she'd started, she stopped. "*Madonna*, it's staring right at me, and I didn't see it. We walked right into it."

"See what?"

"Suzie, you been outta Brooklyn too long." Laying the sponge on the stove, Angie looked her sister in the eye. "It was a plant."

"What kind of a plant?" Bitsy sniffed.

"The gun was planted." Angie rushed to the table and took Bitsy by the shoulders. "It was a setup. Someone didn't put the gun there to hide it—they put it there so it would be found. And we were the *mamalukes* that found it."

"Mama what?"

"Idiots, morons." Plopping into a chair, Angie slapped her palm on her forehead. "We walked right into it."

Bitsy rubbed the tears off her cheeks and sat up. "But how would anyone know we would be there?"

"They didn't know *we* would find it," Angie said. "But it's a cemetery. Even if they didn't know that Travis was going to be buried nearby, someone would have eventually found it."

There was a knock on the door. Apollo began to howl.

Susannah looked from Angie to Bitsy. "We don't talk about this to anyone, got it?"

At the door, Susannah peered through the peephole and shocked to see Varina Withers. She sped to the kitchen. "It's the detective." Deftly plucking her sister out of the chair, she whispered, "Go to your room and stay in there."

Angie ran down the hall, followed by Apollo, who barked loudly. Smoothing her hair, Susannah sailed to the door. Detective Withers gave her a semi-serpentine smile and held out her hand. "Dr. Shine." Her kinky blond hair spilled onto her shoulders, and she wore the windbreaker that she never seemed to be without.

"Detective Withers. Can I help you?"

"Yes. As a matter of fact, I was hoping I could ask you some questions."

As she entered, the clacking of dog nails heralded Apollo's arrival. He gave a weary *woof* and sniffed the detective's khaki pants.

"Oh, you have a dog."

Despite Susannah's effort to reroute the canine, he followed the detective into the kitchen, barking.

"He's my dog." Bitsy patted Apollo's head. "Kind of."

"I'm glad you're here too." Maneuvering around the animal, Detective Withers addressed Bitsy. "I wanted to ask you both a few more questions." The detective pulled her notebook out, and Apollo leapt at it.

"Down, boy." Removing a few pieces of leftover sausage from a dish on the table, Bitsy enticed Apollo away. He fell on the

CHAPTER TWENTY-NINE

sausage and ate with gusto.

"Chief Laughton was first on the scene because he had been in Tussahaw Junction at the time," Detective Withers continued, "but I have some questions."

"I don't know what I can tell you." Butterflies caused a maelstrom in Susannah's stomach. Little Junior had seen Keith being fingerprinted only a few minutes earlier. Accusing Keith must mean that Angie was no longer under suspicion, but Susannah bristled at the thought that this woman wanted her to implicate Keith. "Apollo found the gun and dumped it into the open grave. Randy got there pretty fast after that."

"I'm trying to get a better understanding of what was happening before you...er, Apollo, found the gun."

Bitsy returned for another piece of sausage with Apollo at her heels. The thought of dog slobber and sausage grease on her carpet made Susannah recoil, but she said nothing. "Uh, well, we were at the First Methodist Church in Tussahaw Junction for Travis Keene's funeral service early this morning. Randy knows all this. He was there too."

"I understand that. But I'm after more specific information." She pointed the tip of her pen at Susannah. "Why were you there? Did you know the deceased?"

"Not very well, but he was a member of the Peach Grove Business Association and B—" Susannah turned to point to Bitsy, who was wiping Apollo's mouth with a napkin. "Uh, Ms. Long is president. So I went with her to represent the association."

As the detective jotted some notes, Bitsy tossed the soiled napkin in the trash and went to the sink to wash her hands. Raising her voice to compete with the sound of running water, Detective Withers shot Bitsy a look and asked, "How long did you stay at the church?"

"Maybe ten or fifteen minutes." Susannah glanced at Bitsy. What had Apollo done that caused Bitsy to scrub her fingernails with the vegetable brush? She opened her mouth to ask, but was interrupted by the detective's next question.

"Did you see anything out of the ordinary?"

The room went silent as Bitsy shut off the water and picked up a towel to dry her hands. She said, "If you call a woman wearing a red dress with black-and-white spiky sandals at a funeral *out of the ordinary*, then yes, we did."

The detective shifted her gaze back to Susannah. "I understand Ms. Hibbard showed up somewhat inappropriately dressed for a funeral."

"That's an understatement," Bitsy mumbled, with a look of admiration on her face.

"And her attire caused a disturbance between Ms. Hibbard and the widow, Mrs. Crystal Keene?"

"It was more like cage match with accessories," Bitsy said. "That Crystal is a hot mess."

"But beyond that," the detective continued, "did either of you notice anything else? Anyone who you think shouldn't have been there?"

"No," Bitsy replied quickly, but now that Susannah thought about it, Randy was out of place. She supposed he was there waiting to see if the murderer would show up like they always do in detective shows on TV.

"Like I said…" Susannah trailed off as Apollo lumbered to the sink and looked up at Bitsy, his droopy eyes supplicating her. "What's wrong with him?"

"I don't think he liked Angie's Italian sausage," Bitsy replied. "He's probably more used to Jimmy Dean brand. Aren't you,

CHAPTER TWENTY-NINE

boy?" With a sigh, Apollo lay down with his paws on Bitsy's feet, his tongue hanging out of his mouth.

"He's probably thirsty," Detective Withers observed.

"I was just getting to that." Snatching up a mixing bowl, Bitsy again ran the water. At the sound of the water coming on, Apollo lifted his head.

"Finish your thought, Dr. Shine," Detective Withers said as Bitsy placed the bowl on the floor and Apollo began lustily lapping.

"Oh, well, I was just saying that I didn't know Travis very well." Susannah glanced down at the dog who was still drinking, his jowls in the water. "So I wouldn't have really noticed anyone out of place."

Detective Withers nodded, tapping her pen on her chin. "Chief Laughton says you all left the church with Ms. Hibbard, is that correct?"

"Yes, we followed her out."

"Why?"

"Why?" Susannah was stumped for a moment. "I suppose I sort of chose sides when I helped Maggie pick up her stuff, and I didn't want to get into a confrontation with Crystal."

"I second that emotion." Bitsy held up a finger until the hound's lapping had slowed significantly, and then she directed her gaze at the detective. "I went to show my respect as the president of the Peach Grove Business Association, seeing as how our members had chipped in and bought a floral arrangement. But I didn't have to stick around for the abuse."

"I see." Detective Withers was quiet for a while. "And the three of you went to the cemetery together?"

"No," Susannah said. "I drove with Angie, and Bitsy met us later after she picked up Apollo."

"How long did it take you to pick him up?"

"Only a few minutes," Bitsy answered. "My cousin Kiara lives right there in the Junction. She's lending Apollo out to me for our Growl-A-Ween contest."

"So you drove separately. You and your sister got there first," Detective Withers observed. "Did you see anyone else in the cemetery?"

Susannah shook her head. "Only the gentleman who was setting up the chairs for Travis's funeral."

"No one else?"

"No, uh," Susannah paused. "Well, I did notice one person outside the cemetery on the sidewalk. It was a bit odd because he was wearing a ghost costume."

The detective blinked, and Susannah thought she saw her eye twitch. She immediately looked down and jotted something on her notepad.

"Oh Lord," Bitsy said. "First doppelgangers, now ghosts."

"It was a man." Susannah looked at Bitsy and then at Apollo, who had slumped onto Bitsy's feet. "Is he all right?"

"Kiara says when he's tired, he likes to snooze on shoes." Bitsy grinned.

Susannah rolled her eyes.

"It was a man?" Detective Withers asked.

"He or she was wearing a mask and long black robes, but from the height and build, yes, I thought it was a man."

"What kind of mask?"

"One of those Ghostface masks. Like from the movie—"

"*Scream*," the detective finished.

At the word *scream*, Apollo began to snore.

"Do you think that's important?" Susannah asked.

The detective shrugged. "It seems to be a popular costume

CHAPTER TWENTY-NINE

this year."

Susannah mulled that over as Apollo's snoring got louder. To Bitsy, she said, "That dog must have sleep apnea. You should get him tested."

"No, he's exhausted. He's had a busy day and it's only two o'clock." Bitsy nudged the hound with her foot, and he continued snoring. She rummaged in her purse and found a dog treat. She waved it in front of the hound's face and he opened his eyes. Slowly getting to his feet, he followed Bitsy to the door like the proverbial horse reaching for a carrot on a stick. "We're gonna go."

"A very amusing animal." The detective turned to Susannah. "On a side note, thanks to the discovery of the pistol in the cemetery, your sister's firearm is no longer considered evidence in the case." She handed Susannah a slip of paper. "Angela can call this number to arrange to pick it up."

"You don't really think Keith had anything to do with these murders, do you?"

"I don't base my arrests on what I think. I base them on what the evidence tells me." With that, she turned and headed for the door. "And the evidence tells me he's in deep. I'll let myself out."

CHAPTER THIRTY

Border Business

Angie stamped her feet and blew into her hands.

Susannah asked, "How can you be cold? You've lived in New York your whole life. It's much colder than this in Brooklyn." She lowered herself onto a bale of hay on the sidewalk in front of Peachy Things. Situating herself between a big jack-o'-lantern and a well-dressed scarecrow, she hunkered down in the autumn decorations to wait. Several painted pumpkins sat on the ground, and the tip of her shoe touched the stem of one.

"We've been standing in this doorway for twenty minutes." Angie wrinkled her nose at Susannah. "I don't know why we couldn't have just gone to Bitsy's house. Even if the Peach Grove PD is watching us, we're not giving them any evidence they can use against Keith."

"No, but if they know we're doing our own investigation, they'll try to stop us." Susannah slapped her fist into her hand in exasperation. After Varina Withers had left her house, Susannah noticed a car parked down the road from her house. A call to Bitsy had uncovered the same thing. "Besides, Randy thinks you put the gun there, so I'm not so convinced by the detective's story."

"But where would I have gotten Keith's gun?"

Susannah shook her head. "You've been to Keith and Tina's. You could have stolen it."

"*Mannaggia!*" Raising her hand, she backed into the doorway. "Someone's coming."

They stared as a figure crossed the street and headed their way. It was barely six o'clock, and the sun was beginning to set; in the twilight, Susannah wasn't sure if the person in a long, dark hooded jacket was Bitsy or not. An energetic wave gave her the answer.

"Hey, y'all," Bitsy said, unlocking the door as two bells jangled against the glass. She snapped on the lights as she entered, then turned around. "Whatcha you waiting for? It's cold."

"No foolin'," Angie grumbled.

"I decided to walk," said Bitsy

They piled into the store and Bitsy shut the door.

"How did you get by the squad car without them seeing?" Susannah asked, watching Bitsy carefully.

"I told you the other day." Digging into her hoodie pocket, Bitsy pulled out a small black flashlight. "Maybe you didn't hear me because the Norfolk Southern was passing through. I walked through the woods behind the houses. That's how I found you so fast the other day."

"I knew it!" Susannah exclaimed.

"I know you knew it," Bitsy scolded. "I told you the other day."

"I know, I know." Susannah went to the checkout counter, placed a hand on the earring rack, and stared at the cash register. "I thought you had a computer here."

"I use a laptop now." Bitsy gestured to the curtain that

separated the sales floor from the break room. "It's in the back."

"Let's go." Susannah beckoned to the women, who were not moving fast enough for her. She squeezed between a rack of blouses and a display of purses. "Come on."

"What gives?" Holding the pumpkin-speckled curtain aside for Angie, Bitsy followed. The back room doubled as a storage area for inventory and as a break room where Bitsy could eat her lunch.

"Where's the laptop?" asked Susannah.

Bitsy pointed to the Dell, which was sitting on a half wall next to a small table.

Susannah sat down at the table and said, "I think I finally understand what Crystal meant."

"About what?" Bitsy grabbed the laptop and took it to the table where Susannah sat. The screen came on, and she engaged the browser.

"We need a Google map of Peach Grove."

Bitsy brought up a picture of the Peach Grove Municipal Building next to an equal-sized map. With one click, the city of Peach Grove filled the screen.

Susannah pointed. "Scroll in on Cutz & Curlz. I want to see Maggie's property."

"Okay." Bitsy zoomed in until the property lines were clearly visible. A little teardrop-shaped icon labeled *Cutz & Curlz* appeared over the representation of Maggie's building.

"Now switch to satellite view."

Bitsy touched the square labeled *satellite*, and the map instantly changed from a bright gray to dark green. Suddenly, the screen was filled with an image of trees.

"That's it," Susannah murmured. "That's got to be it."

CHAPTER THIRTY

"What's it?" asked Angie.

"Hang on," Susannah replied. To Bitsy she added, "Toggle to the map view and zoom out a bit."

Bitsy touched the screen again, and Susannah shouted, "Right there!"

Bitsy jumped. Angie swore in Italian. "What's there? I don't see anything."

"That's it exactly. It's hiding in plain sight." Pointing to the rear property line of Cutz & Curlz with a pen, she indicated the lots next to Maggie's salon. Four properties had yards of the same length. "Here's Bitsy's cousin's property. This is Maggie's property, and two houses next door. They all back up to the water authority property."

"Yeah," Bitsy said, "there's a little reservoir over there."

"Right. Now when I first looked at this map, I saw how all these properties back up to public property." She touched the screen, and a mass of trees came into view behind the houses. "Lots of trees but no houses. I couldn't figure out why Travis would hide something on a property that went nowhere. But after the visit from Varina, I got to thinking about what Crystal said." She touched the screen and dragged the map toward them.

"Ya mean about Travis still loving Crystal?" asked Angie. "I don't think—"

"No." Susannah looked at Angie. "The part about him using Maggie."

Bitsy shook her head and made *tsking* sounds under her breath, and Susannah indicated her with a nod of her head. "See, that's what we all thought. That Crystal meant Travis was using Maggie for sex."

"That's what that expression usually means."

"But Travis was using Maggie for her business location." Dragging the map to the left revealed a property two houses down from Bitsy's cousin's, with a long, diagonal property line. The sides of the property ran straight and created a rectangular shape. But one side was much longer than the other, extending at least half a length further. This caused the end of the property to taper and come to a point. Susannah pointed at the lot. "You see that?"

"The trapezoid?" Bitsy asked.

"A trapezoid?" Angie furrowed her brow. "What are you, a geometry nerd?"

"It's like a rectangle, but crooked." Bitsy shrugged. "And I prefer *girl geek*."

"Focus, you two." Susannah shook her finger. "Not the, uh, trapezoid. The house."

They peered at the screen.

"There." Susannah pointed. "Hidden from view and not accessible from Peachtree Street. Except through the trees."

Angie leaned over Bitsy and inspected the screen.

"It would be the perfect place to live if you wanted to be close to town but not be seen coming and going in your vehicle." Susannah sat and looked at Bitsy. "You can't drive there from this side of town, can you?"

"No," Bitsy said, shrinking and dragging the map to get a bird's-eye view of the downtown area. "You have to go down Peachtree Street, past my house 'bout another half mile, and then cut over to Grove Street and come up Walker Drive. But it's probably a five-minute walk from Maggie's."

"Whoever lives there could get to that deer in Maggie's yard anytime and be back home in a few minutes without anyone ever being the wiser. It's the perfect plan if you didn't want

CHAPTER THIRTY

your face seen around Travis's store holding a small item—like a gun."

"Guns," Bitsy said. "A gun or two would fit inside that foam piece."

"Who do you think lives there?" Angie asked.

"I'm not one hundred percent sure, but it seems to be someone who would have access to guns. Someone who drives a really distinct car and has a really distinct face."

"Who do you think it is, Suzie?"

"Owen Chaffin."

CHAPTER THIRTY-ONE

Travesty in the Trees

"Owen Chaffin?" Angie asked. "Who's that?"

"He's a new officer on the job at the Peach Grove PD. He was at the school the night Gus died. And he was with Keith the night we went to the haunted house."

Tapping the screen with her nail, Bitsy asked, "Why do you think he lives there?"

"Because of something he said at Tina and Keith's Halloween party. I remembered seeing him there for a few minutes. I overheard him tell someone his house is on a lot close to town but with so many trees, it's like living in the woods."

"But that could be anywhere," Bitsy said. "Peach Grove is surrounded by trees."

"I know, I know, but think about it."

"What am I thinking about? That I need a hot drink?" Bitsy rolled her chair over to a small refrigerator, removed a pitcher of water, and filled her Keurig coffee maker. "Go on."

"The guns."

"Which guns?" Angie asked, then put a finger up. "I'll have hot chocolate."

"Well, all the guns. Mine, yours, and Keith's."

CHAPTER THIRTY-ONE

"You and Angie bought your guns from Travis." Bitsy placed her coffee on the table and returned to the machine. "You think that's related?"

"Yes, I do. No one has asked why Angie's gun was found at the scene of Gus's death."

"I did," Angie said. "But no one listened to me."

"I kept thinking about the guns and Travis." Susannah put her hands down flat and stared at them. "Then all of a sudden, what Crystal said to Maggie clicked into place. Crystal told Maggie she was just another one of Travis's deals. Once I realized that Crystal wasn't talking about Maggie personally, I knew Travis had to be involved in some kind of scheme to sell guns."

Angie's face fell. "A scheme that involves Owen and Keith?"

"Well, not Keith."

"Not Keith. It would kill Tina." Crossing herself, Angie mumbled the name of Jesus in Italian and took a cup of hot chocolate from Bitsy.

"Did you research the Business Association membership forms?" asked Susannah.

"I sure did," Bitsy replied. "Crystal is not a partner in Travis's store. But that doesn't mean she's not involved in some other kind of illegal deal."

A furrow appeared in Angie's forehead. "But Travis sells guns legally at the store."

"I know, and that's what kept me from focusing on Travis in the first place." Susannah sighed. "I couldn't find his relation to Gus. Then Travis was killed, and Crystal freaked out and got me thinking."

"But how does that tie in with Owen?"

Susannah chewed her lip. "Okay, I'm not sure of all the

details, but it has something to do with Gus asking you about your Glock. You told me it was his idea to change the sights. Right?"

"Right."

"We have to believe that Gus and Travis have some kind of connection. We can talk about that in a minute, but let's just say for now that they knew each other and that Gus was working for or helping Travis."

"Okay?"

"So for some reason, Travis is interested in your gun," Susannah continued. "But he sold you that gun, so what gives?"

"This talking in circles always makes me hungry." Bitsy opened a cabinet and pulled out a package of Pepperidge Farm Milano cookies and shook her finger at Angie, "Now, don't you go into chocolate overload."

Ignoring the rustling of the bag, Susannah continued, "And then it occurred to me. Little Junior told you that there have been lots of closed-door meetings, right?" She didn't wait for Bitsy to answer. "Little Junior usually finds out all kinds of information, but this time he wasn't hearing anything."

Bitsy crunched a Milano cookie and raised her eyebrows, encouraging Susannah to go on.

"Then Tina said Keith seemed distracted and wouldn't talk about it." She pointed at Bitsy. "Little Junior thought the county task forces might be involved. And then I remembered something. When I was in the NYPD, there was one thing that would make doors slam, cops clam up, and outside investigators show up in your precinct."

Angie stopped sipping her hot chocolate and frowned. "You mean Internal Affairs?" Having grown up with a father and older brothers on the police force, both women felt a certain

CHAPTER THIRTY-ONE

amount of dread hearing the term. "You think someone on the force is under investigation?"

Cookie halfway to her mouth, Bitsy gasped. "Keith?"

"Owen."

"How can you be sure?"

"Just listen." Holding her hand up, Susannah counted on her fingers. "Owen Chaffin came from Tussahaw Junction. Travis lived in Tussahaw Junction. Gus's last job was in Tussahaw Junction. I don't know why I didn't see it sooner. They probably all knew each other. Travis and Gus were veterans. I'm not sure about Owen. Gus had a service-related injury, and Crystal said Travis did too. They could have met getting treated at the Atlanta VA Medical Center. And then there was what Doyle said."

"Doyle?"

"Doyle Etheridge, he's a patient of mine. Remember I mentioned him? He was at the funeral."

"The older guy who caught the flying Super Plus." Angie snickered.

"Yes, he grew up in Tussahaw Junction and told me that the woods down there have always attracted criminals. Gangs, drugs, guns."

"But—" Bitsy tried to speak, but Susannah hushed her with a wave of the hand.

"Remember how Crystal put it? *Just another one of Travis's deals.* What if Travis and Owen got together for a deal?"

"What kind of a deal, Suzie?"

"Well, at this point"—lifting one shoulder, Susannah gave a slight shrug—"it's mostly guesswork. Internal investigations happen because of a complaint about an officer's conduct or behavior. They look for corruption, but there's also things like losing evidence."

"Evidence like guns," Bitsy said.

"And drugs," Angie added.

"Yup." Susannah stood. "What if Owen was taking guns from the evidence room and giving them to Travis to sell?"

The women were silent for a moment, and then Bitsy said, "That makes some kind of sense. If Owen wanted to get a gun to Travis, he could just walk through the trees and leave it at Maggie's property. Travis could go by and pick it up, and no one would ever see them together."

"But what about the serial numbers?" Angie asked.

"He could have changed the serial number by one digit when he wrote it up so it wouldn't set off any warnings. If he didn't do it often, no one would notice." Susannah tilted her head. "He and Owen would split a couple hundred bucks. Not bad for someone on a cop's salary."

"Okay." Angie put her mug down. "But how did Keith get mixed up in this?"

"I think when Owen was at Tina and Keith's house, he stole Keith's off-duty weapon and then used it to shoot Travis and Gus. I think he's the one who planted it in the cemetery."

"How are we going to prove all this?" asked Angie.

"I have a plan."

"Of course you do," said Bitsy.

CHAPTER THIRTY-TWO

A Peachy Plan

During the next half hour, Susannah ran her plan by Bitsy and Angie. She wasn't sure she needed their approval, but she did need their help. Detective Withers's focus was off Angie, so she felt like she could breathe a little easier on that matter. But with Keith's head on the chopping block, she needed to move soon. Tapping her pen on her knee, she pondered what kind of evidence she could bring to Randy and Detective Withers that would convince them her theory was correct. At this point, she wasn't even sure what she was looking for. Perusing the coffee pods that Bitsy kept in a metallic drawer under the coffee maker, she chose the only dark roast, one called Laughing Man Colombian. She watched it drip while eavesdropping on Bitsy.

Bitsy's first call had been to her cousin LaDonna Long, who now worked at the city water department. LaDonna verified from memory that Owen Chaffin lived in a house on Walker Drive. Perhaps not one hundred percent reliable information, but Susannah felt it confirmed her suspicions, and she gave a small whoop followed by a tiny fist pump.

Bitsy quirked an eyebrow. "You can do better than that."

Dance ability was not something Susannah was gifted with, but she lifted one knee in an exaggeration of The Twist.

"Please don't." Bitsy closed her eyes and sighed before texting Little Junior. He confirmed that Owen Chaffin would be on duty the next morning, directing traffic at the start of the Peach Grove Halloween festivities.

"Just what are you going to do?" Angie wrung her hands. "If you're right, this guy is dangerous."

"Ange, I owe Keith and Tina."

"I know you do, but there has to be a safer way." A lock of hair dropped over Angie's forehead, and she pushed it out of the way. "Talk to Randy first. Or you can hire a private detective. Like Tone. He might take the case."

Tone was Anthony Mancuso, Susannah's former partner on the NYPD. He had retired from New York to Florida and opened his own business as a private investigator.

"It won't be dangerous." The coffee finished brewing, and Susannah added milk to the cup. "I'm just going to check out Owen's house while he's busy with the parade." Her phone vibrated. "It's Maggie. I need to take this." With the phone on speaker, she wandered into Peachy Things's showroom, commiserating with Maggie over the unfairness of losing Travis in such a devastating way.

"It was horrible enough that he died," Maggie's voice quavered, "but the humiliation of finding out he had been cheating on me with his own wife…well, that put me over the edge. In a weird way," she continued, "it's like I became a widow and a mistress, all on the same day. I can't show my face in public anymore. Especially not after the Tampax affair."

Bitsy snatched the phone out of Susannah's hand. "Miss Maggie, never you mind about all that. Now everyone knows

CHAPTER THIRTY-TWO

that Travis was a cheater, and Crystal is loony tunes. If Travis Keene was here today, it would serve him right if you killed him."

The guffaws that came through the phone were loud enough to be heard across the room. Bitsy gave Susannah a thumbs-up. "Anyway, I could use your help with the Growl-A-Ween Parade tomorrow morning. Why don't you meet me at Peachy Things in the morning? The Peach Grove Business Association needs you."

There was silence as Bitsy switched off the speaker and brought the phone to her ear. "Well, no," she told Maggie, "I don't think holding a boycott of a member's store is allowed." She looked at Angie and Susannah and twirled her finger in a circle at her temple, the universal sign for *this chick is bonkers.*

Susannah grabbed the phone. Before the call ended, she had secured the use of Maggie's parking lot while the Growl-A-Ween Parade was on. Maggie even agreed to double-check Owen's address since he had come in to get a haircut a few times. "So it's all set," she told Angie and Bitsy. "Tomorrow while the police block off traffic, and the Growl-A-Ween Parade starts, I'll do some snooping around. You two make sure that Owen is kept busy so I have time to get over there and look around."

Angie sighed. "I hope it's as easy as that."

"Don't worry. What could go wrong?"

CHAPTER THIRTY-THREE

Susannah gets the Boot

The next morning dawned overcast. Steam filled the shower as Susannah went over her plan for the day. By tonight, she was sure she would have evidence pointing to Owen as the killer, and Keith and Angie would be in the clear. Confidence filled her. As part of her plan, she had chosen a camouflage outfit as a Halloween costume. Described by both Angie and Bitsy as "super cute," it had the added benefit of aiding her on her stealth mission to find Owen Chaffin's house. If he did live where she suspected, it would be easy for him to access the faux deer at the salon. Even Randy would be able to see the connection.

Susannah peeped into Caden's bedroom where a scene from *Star Wars Episode IV: A New Hope* replayed itself. Angie, dressed as Princess Leia in long white robes, bent over Caden, touching his shoulder to wake him. In the darkened room, the glare from his night light against her white robes gave her a halo. The buns only added to the effect.

"C'mon, buddy." Angie shook Caden's shoulder. "Let's get going. I'm already dressed." She looked over at Susannah. "He's eager to see dogs in costumes, but not as eager to get out of

CHAPTER THIRTY-THREE

bed."

"That's okay, we have time." In the kitchen, Princess Leia had put on the coffee, and Susannah grabbed a cup. They had promised to meet Bitsy at seven thirty to help her set up the registration booth and lay out the signs marking the parade route. Caden soon appeared in the kitchen with Angie behind him.

"Here, take this." Angie handed Caden a muffin and reached into the fridge for a juice box.

Susannah's eyebrows went up.

"No lecturing me about high-carb meals. At least it's gluten-free." She prodded Caden toward the door, and they stepped outside.

Humid air smacked Susannah in the face. "Ugh."

"What's wrong, Aunt Suzie?"

"Nothing, sweetie, I just feel a bad hair day coming on."

Caden giggled and mussed his newly combed hair. "I'm having a bad hair day too."

She glanced at her sister, then winked at Caden. "Why aren't you having a bad hair day too?"

"Lots of product."

As they arrived at Peachy Things, Bitsy was parking her SUV. She, Jamal, and Apollo all wore Sherlock Holmes capes and deerstalker caps. Andrea, who had been pressed into service to help watch the boys, wore a T-shirt and yoga pants. Jamal examined Caden's Jedi robes through the cheap plastic lens of a huge magnifying glass. They giggled.

"Don't forget, Jamal has a game later on," Andrea said.

"I remember." Bitsy took her car key off the fob. "Just take my SUV when you need it."

Andrea led Jamal and Caden through the store and out the

back door to the park, which was located behind the strip of stores. The parade would end in the park, where participants would be freed of their canine costumes and allowed to wander in the grass.

Taking a few signs each, Susannah and Angie situated them along the quarter-mile parade route. They set up the registration table where dog parents would sign in and their fur babies would receive a number like they were running the Atlanta Marathon.

As the time ticked down, Susannah nervously gazed down the street and tapped her pocket, where she had placed a printout of the Google map. She gave Bitsy a wave and backtracked to her Jeep. She drove down Main Street toward Peachtree Street and Cutz & Curlz. In her rearview mirror, she watched two Peach Grove PD squad cars pull up; Randy and Owen got out. Her heart thumped in her chest even though she knew there would be little danger while Owen was busy at work.

As Susannah parked at Cutz & Curlz, Maggie opened the door and stepped out, sending Otis, her black and white cat, cowering under a bush. Susannah almost didn't recognize her at first. Though she was in the same red dress she'd worn for Travis's funeral, her face was a deathly white and her eyes were circled with maroon-red shadow, giving her an otherworldly, vampire-like appearance. Her hair trailed down in fanciful twists and curls that adhered to her face like a sculpture.

"Holy cow," Susannah murmured as she approached.

"You like?" Maggie curtsied, holding the skirt out. The same zebra-striped sandals with the four-inch heels graced her feet. "Us stylists are good with hair. And I'll never be able to wear this dress again without thinking about flying Super Plus, so

CHAPTER THIRTY-THREE

the bloody eye makeup is appropriate."

Susannah indicated her approval. "How can you walk in those heels?"

"Practice." Maggie grinned, handing Susannah a slip of paper. "I'm driving to Bitsy's. Not much walking after that. There's Owen's address. We'll keep him busy."

Stuffing the paper into a small backpack, Susannah climbed into her Jeep and headed down Peachtree Street. It was eight o'clock. According to Bitsy's timetable, the roads would be blocked off at eight thirty, and the parade would start at nine. That gave her over an hour to get to Owen's house and back. Easy peasy. She placed Owen's address in her GPS and found the drive exactly as Bitsy had described. Down Peachtree Street to a cross street, then left and left again onto Walker Drive, Owen's road. Susannah thrust her chest out. Maybe she should apply for a private investigator's license. "Get over yourself," she murmured, mashing the button to turn on the radio. "All you did was read a map."

The pavement soon ended, and she slowed the Jeep as she took in the wooded landscape. A few houses dotted the road, and all were hemmed in on three sides by trees. Owen's house was exactly where she thought it would be. Pulling into the driveway, she wondered why they even bothered with the fake deer ploy. It was plenty deserted here. Glancing at the clock, she jumped out of the Jeep. It had taken ten minutes to drive here from Cutz & Curlz. Owen was still working, directing traffic at the Growl-A-Ween Parade. There would be more than enough time to snoop around. A branch rustled, and she surveyed Owen's yard to see a bushy-tailed squirrel climbing a spindly pine.

She group-texted Angie and Bitsy. "I'm here." Bitsy messaged a thumbs-up, but Angie did not reply.

Susannah stepped into the cement drive and crossed to the house. The front yard was small but tidy, the road silent. After knocking on the front door, she tried the knob, but it was locked. Peeking into a window, she made out a family room with a couch, a TV, and a recliner. Standard furnishings. Nothing here screamed *dirty cop*. She walked around the house, checking the windows and rear door. The backyard was small, with patches of scraggly crabgrass and hard-packed dirt. The woods were quiet, and she took a few steps into the trees, wondering if she should bother hiking to Maggie's salon.

Suddenly, music came through the trees, and she stopped and tilted her head, laughing. "Monster Mash." Bitsy's favorite Halloween tune was being played at the parade. That settled it. This property was as close to downtown as she and Bitsy had thought.

Her theory was correct. Except for one slight problem. There was absolutely *no* evidence here. No clues of illegal doings. Nothing to suggest that Owen even lived here. Her mouth, which had been dry before, now felt parched, and she walked to the side of the house, where she had seen a garden hose neatly stowed on a reel mounted on the house. Picking up the hose, she twisted the spigot, allowing an easy trickle of water. A few drops leaked out where the hose attached to the spigot and splattered her boots. She stepped back and drank, the cool water soothing her throat. One final sip and she shut off the faucet and hung the hose back up. Glancing down, she noticed a fresh-looking footprint in the soft soil next to the house.

She bent low and peered at the impression.

A chill went down her spine. It was a bootprint identical to

CHAPTER THIRTY-THREE

the hikers Crystal wore.

CHAPTER THIRTY-FOUR

Downspout Dodge

Susannah froze, her mouth full of water, and listened intently. Was Crystal here?

The air was still. Even the sounds of "Monster Mash" had faded away. Forcing the water down, she eyed the quickest way to the Jeep. She had seen no traces of anyone else around, but she was staring at a fresh footprint in the mud.

It had to be a coincidence. Why would Crystal be at Owen's house now? Taking no chances, she pulled her keys from her back pocket and clutched them. Grabbing her backpack, she unzipped the top and placed her right hand on her Glock. She was not going to be taken unawares.

Hugging the side of the house, she tiptoed to the front yard and peered around the edge of the house. Her car was still the only one in sight, but something seemed out of place. Inhaling slowly, she stepped around the rain gutter as a flash of movement caught her eye.

Crystal was standing on Owen's brick porch, holding a gun. "Stop right there."

Susannah would do no such thing. As she sped down the side of the house, the sound of a bullet shattering wood shingles

CHAPTER THIRTY-FOUR

propelled her along. Wresting her Glock free from its Velcro strap, she ran, her mind racing. She didn't want to die in a shootout with a crazy woman. The sound of Crystal's shoes on the brick porch let her know the woman was on the move. Could she outrun her?

She flung herself around the back of the house as another shot sailed past. Her heart hammered, keys clutched in a damp hand. Could she beat Crystal around the house and get into her Jeep? As the front of the property came into view, her heart sank. The Jeep sat at an odd angle, two tires flat.

A noise came from behind her. Propelled forward by a horrible sense of dread, she scampered around the house and leaped onto the front porch. Mirroring the action Crystal had taken just moments before, she quickly jumped down the other side and scurried behind the aluminum downspout where all this had begun. Having circled the house in what felt like seconds, she sucked in a breath and glanced across the street. Past the trees, she made out a pickup truck parked behind some wild privet bushes. Crystal.

With no neighboring homes deeper in the woods, it was just her and Crystal.

She jammed her keys into her pocket. Both hands now free, she gripped her Glock and racked the slide. Time seemed to slow as she listened for Crystal to come around the front of the house. But she heard nothing. Suddenly, the hair on her neck stood up, and she spun as Crystal rounded the back of the house, gun in hand.

Susannah shot, and shot again. She was sure her aim was wild, but Crystal fell and crawled behind the corner of the house. Susannah sprinted across the yard and into the woods to Crystal's pickup. She threw open the door and cheered out loud when she saw the keys in the ignition. Thank goodness for small-town habits. She jumped in the pickup and sped off.

CHAPTER THIRTY-FIVE

Schrödinger's Crystal

Drumming his fingers on his desk, Randy scowled. Detective Withers pushed her hands deep into the pockets of her khaki pants and said, "Tell me again."

Susannah rolled her eyes. "I've already told you three times. I found out where Officer Chaffin lives and went to his house to look around. While I was looking around, Crystal Keene flattened the tires on my Jeep and then shot at me. I shot back, and I might have hit her."

"And then she lent you her truck to come here," Detective Withers said placidly.

Susannah knew what she must look like after the chase around the house. Her hair was wild and her camouflage T-shirt was smudged with dirt and white streaks of paint from the downspout. "I ran into the woods to get away from her and saw her truck. I thought she might have left a spare key somewhere." She shrugged, suddenly feeling exhausted. "But the keys were in the ignition, so I jumped in and left."

"That's some story, Doctor," the detective said.

There was a knock on the door, and Detective Withers opened it. Susannah ignored the whispered conversation and sipped at cold coffee from a Styrofoam cup. If they were going to arrest her for trespassing, they should get on with it. She didn't think they would charge her with interfering with an investigation because there didn't seem to be any interest in investigating Owen. When she'd first suggested that Owen could have known Travis and Gus, Randy ground his teeth so hard she thought a vein would burst in his neck. Detective Withers's bored expression hadn't changed much, and Susannah soon felt ridiculous for mentioning it.

At the door, the detective waved for Randy to follow her. As he passed Susannah, he placed his hand on her shoulder. "Stay here. I'll have someone bring you fresh coffee."

Susannah pulled her phone from her backpack and found twelve messages from Bitsy and three from Angie. She sent a quick thumbs-up to their *Everything okay?* messages. As she had careened down the dirt road in Crystal's F-150, she had been terrified that Crystal would dive into the street and take potshots at her. That hadn't happened, and she didn't know if Crystal was lying behind Owen's house, wounded, or if she had crawled away to hide. When Susannah got to the Peach Grove PD, Little Junior had stopped her midstory and walked her straight to Randy's office. Too terrified to use her phone while in the truck, she was playing catch-up now.

There was a tap on the door, and Little Junior entered with a steaming Styrofoam cup. As he leaned in to hand it to her, he whispered, "I texted Bitty for you."

Susannah suppressed a laugh. She had forgotten that Bitsy's Aunt Eunice called her Bitty, and Little Junior followed suit. "Thanks." She waved her phone at him. "I'm answering her now." Sipping at the bitter coffee, she pondered how to explain to Bitsy and Angie that her plan had backfired. As she stared at her phone, collecting her thoughts, Randy returned alone, shutting the door behind him.

His gaze riveted on her, he placed his hands on the back of his chair. "Dr. Shine, I want you to know that we have taken your report and sent a car out to check on your story. An officer searched the property, and there was no sign of Ms. Keene. We'll keep an eye out for her. Your Jeep was found with two flat tires, so the officer had it towed. You can pick it up this afternoon from the city impound lot." He leaned across the desk and handed her a sheet of paper with the address and phone number of the lot.

Waiting for more, Randy just gazed at her. "That's it?" she asked. "What about the bullet hitting the house? There must be some evidence of that."

Randy's light blue eyes turned gray. His voice pitched louder than Susannah thought was necessary. "*I said* we have all we need. You can go." There was that jaw grinding again. He came around his desk and pulled open the door. As the door momentarily wedged him into the corner of the room, he raised his eyebrows and whispered, "For your own safety, don't talk about this." He threw the door wide and folded his arms.

Across the room, an officer she didn't know stared at her. She folded the sheet of paper and pushed it into her pocket. The muscles in her neck stiffened as she thought about Crystal. If they hadn't found her at Owen's place, that meant that she was on the loose somewhere. Susannah stopped. How had Crystal gotten away without her truck?

Little Junior gave her a nod. "Doctor."

She left the building half expecting Bitsy to greet her from her SUV, but the parking lot was deserted. A sour taste settled in her mouth as she thought about warning Bitsy and

Maggie. Even more urgent, she had to get Angie and Caden home as soon as possible. Across the parking lot and past the municipal building, she trudged head down. On Main Street, she met more decorative scarecrows and costumed canines. A Pekingese in a red wig and *Little Mermaid* tail yapped at her. She scanned the street for Owen and Crystal but didn't see either. There wasn't any police presence at all. That was not a good sign. Phone in hand, she checked the time, disoriented when she realized it was almost three o'clock. How long had she been at the police station?

At Peachy Things, Bitsy ran to her, her Sherlock Holmes cape flapping. "Where have you been?"

Susannah looked around. "Where's Angie and Caden?"

Bitsy looked out the window, craning her neck to see around the scarecrow that was blocking the view. "Over there." She pointed toward the Scarecrow Village, which had been set up on the green space across from her shop. "The Trunk-or-Treating is all finished, and Caden wanted to look for Apollo." Pouting, she hung her head. "That's the last place we saw that bad dog after he stole a little boy's candy and ran off."

"I bet you're wishing for squirrels right now."

Bitsy grinned. "Except for the Apollo incident, Growl-A-Ween was a success. Miss Shirleen Carter won the costume contest. She was dressed as Dorothy from *The Wizard of Oz* and her dog, Jack—"

"Don't tell me," Susannah interrupted, "he was dressed as Toto."

"Now how could a boxer pull off a Toto costume?" Bitsy asked, her hands on her hips. "He was dressed as the Tin Man. He had a cute little funnel hat."

Susannah smiled.

CHAPTER THIRTY-FIVE

"Kinda like Apollo's deerstalker cap." Bitsy teared up. "Only we never got to the costume contest because he ran away. He was my practice puppy and he ran away. I'm a terrible fur parent."

It was Susannah's turn to comfort her friend. She gave her a hug and patted her back. "It's okay, it's not your fault. He was probably hungry."

"I know." Bitsy sniffed. "His psoriasis meds give him a big appetite."

Over her shoulder, Susannah looked out the window to see Angie holding Caden's hand as they wandered through the Scarecrow Village. Caden, wearing the light brown Jedi costume with a dark brown hooded robe, blended into the straw and autumn-themed colors. Angie's flowing white Princess Leia robes stuck out.

"We've got to get this dog search on the road." Susannah gave Bitsy one final pat and backed up, holding her at arm's length. "Crystal was at Owen's house and took a shot at me."

"Crackers Crystal. I knew she was dangerous."

"Let's find Apollo and get everyone home."

CHAPTER THIRTY-SIX

Canine Canter

Across the street in the Scarecrow Village, Angie and Caden were doing a cursory search of the straw men for any sign of Apollo. Susannah kept an eye out for Crystal.

"Where's Owen?" asked Susannah.

"The police left as soon as the Growl-A-Ween parade was over." Bitsy jerked her thumb over her shoulder. "The Trunk-or-Treat don't need a police presence."

"I'm not sure Owen's our killer."

"What about the Tussahaw Junction connection?" Bitsy fingered a small rubber mouse that sat on a hay bale, part of the Pest Arrest Extermination Company's display. It incorporated a scarecrow who stood upright via a thick stake and wore a back pack pesticide sprayer. The scare-pest-control-man pointed a nozzle at the bale.

Susannah thought. "Yeah, that still makes sense. But then why was Crystal shooting at me?"

Picking up a rubber bat from the display, Bitsy flapped its wings in Susannah's face. "'Cause she's batty?"

"Suzie." Angie drew near, a hay bale snagging her Princess

CHAPTER THIRTY-SIX

Leia robes. "Where ya been?"

"I'll tell you later." Susannah fingered the zipper on her backpack as she watched Angie tug her robes free. The flowing fabric had dirt and hay stuck to the hem. Caden's trousers had also suffered a couple of stains. "Let's help Bitsy find Apollo and get out of here."

"Go look under that table for Apollo," Angie told Caden, pointing at the display the coffee shop had set up, a scarecrow sitting at a table holding a huge wooden fork and spoon. Susannah had seen an identical fork and spoon set decorating the wall of her nana's kitchen. Otis, Maggie's cat, sat on the hay bale next to the scarecrow licking his paw.

"We looked under there already," Caden said.

"Look again." As Caden walked away, Angie whispered, "I was worried about you."

"I'm okay. I'll tell you everything later. We have to find the dog and get out of here." Susannah knew she should tell Angie the whole story, but she didn't want to frighten her or Caden. They would be okay for now, out in the open with other people strolling down Main Street. At least she knew that Crystal wasn't hiding under a hay bale ready to attack her with a gigantic wooden spoon. She walked over to Caden.

"Come on, Caden, I'll help you." She extended her hand to Caden, and they walked to the table and searched under it. "I don't see any Sherlock Hound," Susannah said.

"Sherlock Hound." Giggling, Caden capered over to Bitsy. "Did you hear that, Miss Bitsy? Aunt Suzie called Apollo 'Sherlock Hound.' That's funny."

"I heard her," Bitsy huffed.

"How come you're not laughing?"

"'Cause I wish I had thought of it first." Bitsy winked at

Caden. "Let's keep looking. By the way." Bitsy turned to Angie, who was picking straw out of her Princess Leia buns. "Where are Jamal and Andrea?"

"Andrea took Jamal to his game."

Susannah felt relieved—Crystal didn't know Andrea and Jamal, so Susannah didn't have to worry about their safety. As she scanned the second row of scarecrows, her gaze settled on a hay bale; she jabbed Caden in the ribs and he giggled. "Hey." She touched his shoulder and gently turned him. "I think that hay bale is moving."

Together they walked over, a jerky snore now audible. Susannah peeked over the bale. One of Apollo's ears was visible.

Caden laughed. "Apollo, it's Apollo!" He stamped his feet and pointed. "Hey, boy."

Apollo woke with a growl and a woof, and Otis the cat looked up, paw raised mid-groom. Apollo sat up, sniffed the air and barked, deerstalker still on his head. Launching off the coffee shop display, Otis dislodged the spoon, which fell into the scarecrow, knocking it over. Otis shot up in the air, his fur looking like every caricature of a Halloween black cat Susannah had ever seen. Caden laughed and pointed as Otis flew down the street.

Apollo charged the cat at warp speed. As he passed Bitsy, she reached out, missing the dog but snagging his cape. The deerstalker remained steadfast as he continued through the Scarecrow Village and down the street. Otis sprinted across the railroad tracks toward Cutz & Curlz.

Caden tried to follow Apollo, but Susannah stopped him. "No," she told him, "you stay with your mom." She walked him over to Angie. "Do me a favor, go wait with Caden at Peachy

CHAPTER THIRTY-SIX

Things." Angie gave her a look, but Susannah squeezed Angie's arm. "Please. I will explain once we get this dog. I don't want Caden running around where he might get away from us."

Taking Caden by the shoulders, Angie muttered, "Okay."

Susannah watched them cross the street and then followed Bitsy, who was hustling across the railroad tracks after Apollo. When she'd finally caught up, Susannah joined Bitsy in front of Cutz & Curlz, huffing. "Where did they go?"

Bent over, Apollo's cape hanging from her wrist, Bitsy made a motion with her head and straightened. "Over. There." Apollo had made it up the stairs onto the wraparound porch but had apparently pooped out and was lying with his head on his paws, panting. Susannah climbed the stairs, gave the pooch a pat, and then planted herself next to him. Bitsy followed suit and perched on the porch on the other side of the dog. Throwing his rumpled cape over her shoulder, she grasped his collar. "I got you now, you little scoundrel."

"When did I get so out of shape?" Susannah panted along with Apollo.

"I think we've been over this before. Angie. Muffins. Lasagna." Bitsy plopped her bag onto the porch and began rummaging through it. The porch creaked, and Susannah searched for the black cat, but he was nowhere to be seen.

"What are you doing?"

"Looking for his leash." Bitsy glanced at Susannah and then back into her bag. "I know it's in here."

"Well, why did you take it off him?"

"It clashed with his cape."

"Of course," Susannah replied, trying not to voice the exasperation she felt with her friend. They needed to get back to Main Street. For some reason, the deserted shop was giving her the willies. As Apollo yawned, Susannah grasped Apollo's collar. "I've got him. Maybe you should dump that thing out."

Bitsy gave Susannah a nod and dug deeper into her bag. Suddenly, Apollo's ears came to attention and he began to emit a low whine. Gooseflesh rose on Susannah's arms, and she turned to check behind her. Maggie Hibbard stood at the corner of the house, looking tentatively around the corner.

"Maggie?" Susannah asked. Maggie beckoned with one hand but shook her head almost imperceptibly. A look of pain crossed her face.

"Ah-ha," Bitsy said, removing the leash and holding it up. Susannah nudged her. "What?"

Maggie stepped around the corner. Crystal Keene held a gun to her head.

CHAPTER THIRTY-SEVEN

Blasted Bits & Batting Cleanup

A pollo cleaned Susannah's hand of blasted bits of his doggie treats, which had exploded from Bitsy's concealed-carry purse along with the bullet. Her ears were still ringing, but she had no problem seeing the blue flashing lights of Randy Laughton's Peach Grove Police Department squad car. She watched with satisfaction as Crystal was perp-walked down the front path and shoved into the back door of the patrol car.

Maggie appeared at the salon door carrying two mugs. "Coffee?" she shouted.

"Thanks." The mug was decorated with different-colored scissors, and Susannah raised it to Maggie, then sipped. Maggie sat down next to her on the porch. Together, they watched Randy pull into the street and drive toward downtown Peach Grove. Apollo sighed and lay down on his side, apparently exhausted by his performance as an attack hound. Covering the pooch with the Sherlock Holmes cape, Maggie chuckled. Susannah remembered her opinion of Maggie from the camp-out. A lot had changed in a short period of time, and a lot more probably would.

Suddenly she felt homesick for Angie and Caden.

On the lawn, Bitsy's cousins, Tiffany Long Roberts and her husband, Terrell Roberts, were speaking with Detective Withers. Despite being at the epicenter of the eardrum-injuring blast, Bitsy had her arms around both of them, nodding and encouraging them as if she could hear everything they said. Susannah doubted that she could.

Terrell Roberts's shotgun had appeared through the spindles of Maggie's porch, taking the last bit of fight out of Crystal. Tiffany had already dialed 911, and they both kept watch over Crystal while Susannah, Maggie, and Bitsy calmed Apollo and each other.

Apollo whined in his sleep, and Susannah appraised him, nudging Maggie at the same time. "You hear that?" Susannah pointed at Apollo.

"I did." Maggie leaned in. "I don't think my hearing was damaged as much as yours."

On the lawn, the detective flipped her notebook closed, an action Susannah had noted on other occasions and knew meant she was finished asking questions. Taking her cousins by the hand, Bitsy walked them to their house as Detective Withers turned and faced Cutz & Curlz before asking, "You want to go first?"

Staring into her cup, Maggie didn't look up. Susannah tapped her hand, and Maggie gave her a side-eye glance, tears spilling down her cheek.

"It's gonna be okay," said Susannah.

Maggie nodded and scampered down the wooden steps—now in a pair of white sneakers. Susannah watched her lean toward Detective Withers, cupping her ear with her hand.

"This is going to be fun to watch," Susannah said as Bitsy sat

CHAPTER THIRTY-SEVEN

down in Maggie's place.

"What?" Bitsy asked, cupping her ear with her hand.

Susannah shook her head. "Never mind."

"Speak up, I can't hear you."

Susannah wrapped her arm around Bitsy's shoulder. "I know."

***

At Peachy Things, Bitsy slumped in her chair, one hand around a mug of hot cocoa. Angie and Caden were safe, and Andrea and Jamal had returned from his baseball game blissfully unaware of the trouble. Complaining about rumbling tummies, Angie and Andrea had piled into Bitsy's SUV with the boys and left in search of food. Susannah hadn't even nagged them about eating healthy.

"Let's get going."

Maggie, whose stylish tendrils now hung about her head like knotted ropes, had agreed to take Susannah to the city impound lot to retrieve the Jeep. Bitsy nudged Apollo with her foot. Apollo had been the least affected by the gunshots, snoozing happily on the porch while Detective Withers had questioned everyone involved. The only thing that seemed to energize the pooch, besides a hunk of bad guy thigh, was Otis the cat.

"Fine." Bitsy stood and stretched. "But only if you promise to take me to America's Finest."

"Okay, okay." Susannah had tried to talk Bitsy out of replacing her concealed-carry bag immediately, but she was not having it. She didn't even care that Travis was behind all the chaos that had happened in the last week.

"I'm not going anywhere without my friends Smith & Wesson." Bitsy's purse was in tatters, but her wallet had miraculously survived the live ammo test. She shook the purse in Susannah's direction. "And If I learned anything today, it's that a woman needs plenty of room in her handbag to rack a slide."

"I get it." Susannah put a hand out to Maggie, who moved slowly.

"I'm gonna feel this tomorrow."

"We all are."

Less than an hour later, Susannah found herself in the checkout line at America's Finest with the conveyor belt piled high with Bitsy's purchases. She gazed at the boxes of ammo stacked next to a new pair of sound-canceling earmuffs that must have weighed five pounds. Maggie waited patiently outside the store, Apollo's leash in one hand, a brand-new wooden baseball bat in the other. She had also purchased a concealed-carry handbag—reserved, she said, for future use.

"Apollo sure has taken a shine to Miss Maggie." Bitsy waved at her through the plate glass. Apollo wagged his tail.

"I think she may have fed him a few of Miss Shirleen's cookies," Susannah observed.

"Well, he don't seem none the worse for it."

"No—" Bumped from behind, Susannah was propelled closer to Bitsy. Over her shoulder, a Ghostface mask appeared. Bitsy gasped. The cashier raised her hands as Ghostface brandished a gun.

"Give me all your cash," he mumbled. The cashier was frozen in place. "Now!"

As the cashier fumbled with the register, Susannah stared at the conveyor belt. The voice was familiar. She peeked up at

CHAPTER THIRTY-SEVEN

him. The black robes and creepy mask sent a chill down her neck. Glancing down at his shoes, she noticed a small green leaf stuck to the robes. Bitsy had stiffened but now Susannah felt her relax.

Nudging Bitsy gently, Susannah wanted to yell, *Don't do anything foolish.* But she couldn't and hoped BFF telepathy would work instead.

Not one to mind verbal commands, let alone telepathic ones, Bitsy shifted her weight, ignoring Susannah's extrasensory plea.

As the Ghostface gunman reached for the cash, Susannah ducked, and Bitsy smashed his hand with one hundred rounds of nine-millimeter ammo. He cried out and dropped the gun. Susannah bashed him in the face with the sound-canceling earmuffs, which hit the plastic mask with a *whap*. There was a dull *thwack*, and he staggered back and crumpled.

Maggie stood behind him, clutching her new Louisville Slugger. "I always liked batting cleanup."

As the sound of sirens rose in the distance, Susannah squatted and stripped the gunman of his mask.

Owen Chaffin blinked, his face contorted in pain.

* * *

For the second time that day, Susannah found herself staring down the notepad of Detective Varina Withers. Still clutching her baseball bat, Maggie gave her statement to Randy. Outside the store, Bitsy waited on her cousin Kiara.

"Are you certain you didn't see Mr. Chaffin enter the store?"

Susannah shook her head. "No, he was suddenly behind me."

As Detective Withers inked up her pad, Susannah bit her lip.

"You don't think he was following me, do you?"

"Why do you ask?"

"There was someone in a Ghostface mask at the haunted house, when my purse was stolen. And outside the cemetery when we…" She glanced out the window where Bitsy's cousin Kiara was cuddling Apollo. "When, uh, Apollo found the gun. He must have planted it there."

"I couldn't say," the detective said, but the way her eye twitched gave Susannah the response she needed.

"I knew I was right about him." Susannah glared at the detective. "When I came to you for help, you treated me like I was crazy."

"We took your complaint about Mrs. Keene very seriously." The twitch was gone. Under her breath, but loud enough for Susannah to hear, the detective said, "We can never comment on an ongoing investigation."

"I—"

"That will be all, Doctor." The detective clicked her pen, but this time she didn't flip her pad closed. "I'll be in touch."

As the detective walked away, Maggie approached, her interview with Randy complete. Susannah took her arm. "What was all that about how Owen got in the store?"

"He came out of the storeroom."

"What?" Susannah studied the parking lot, realizing that none of the vehicles belonged to Owen.

"You were right." Maggie raised her voice so it would carry, and Randy glanced at Susannah with a sheepish expression. Maggie huffed out of the store, and Susannah followed. "About Owen and Travis, I mean. Owen must have a key to the employee entrance. It's lucky I saw him come out of the storeroom, or they would be blaming us again."

CHAPTER THIRTY-SEVEN

"I don't think—"

"Hmmph. I don't think the Peach Grove PD has handled this situation well," Maggie continued. "You had it all figured out, but they let cray-cray Crystal and immoral Owen roam the streets. But I never thought Owen would stick up Travis's store," Maggie spat. "Band of brothers, my foot."

Randy approached. "Now, Maggie, we do what we can with the evidence we have."

"Well," Bitsy interjected, "I hope all y'all agree the evidence says Keith can come home."

"No comment."

CHAPTER THIRTY-EIGHT

Stuffed Shells and Bombshells

Susannah pulled a tray of Angie's pepperoni lasagna out of the oven, closing the oven door with her hip. Steam escaped from under the aluminum foil. She placed the tray on the stove and pulled back the foil. Mozzarella cheese resisted the unveiling, sticking to the foil and making dancing strings of cheese. Applause broke out from the kitchen table where Keith, Tina, Bitsy, and Larraine sat. After centering several trivets in the middle of the table, Angie took a bow as her creation took center stage.

"*Mangia!*" Angie said.

Keith stood, his six-foot-five frame towering over the table, and gave Susannah a hug. "I don't know how to thank you, Dr. Shine."

"Leave some for the rest of us." Susannah smiled as Tina got out of her seat and joined in the hug.

"I'm serious," Keith said. "This is the second time you've saved my family. I might need to hire you as a nanny so you can protect the baby."

The doorbell rang, and Angie left the table to answer it.

"You don't really think that detective would have pressed

CHAPTER THIRTY-EIGHT

charges against you, do you?" Larraine asked. "Didn't they have evidence against Owen?"

Keith's face fell. "They had evidence, but nothing directly linking Owen to the thefts from the evidence room." He took Tina's hand and kissed her on the forehead. "He managed to disable the security camera every time there was a theft. When I reported that my off-duty weapon had gone missing after the Halloween party, they thought I was building some sort of cover."

Tina paled a bit, her brown eyes losing their sparkle. She smacked Keith's arm. "Why didn't you tell me about that?"

Keith ushered his wife into her chair, giving her belly a gentle pat and pushing her chair in. "I didn't want you to worry." He sat and looked across the table. "I never thought after my years on the force that Randy would think I was capable of something like that."

"Without evidence, Randy didn't want to accuse anyone of breaking into Keith's gun safe," Tina offered, picking up a piece of Italian bread and buttering it. "And Owen flew under the radar because he'd been in Peach Grove less than a year. And because of how young he is. But he's a lowlife scum."

"No, that lying dog Travis Keene is the real scum." Maggie Hibbard clopped into the kitchen behind Angie, wearing leather pants and stiletto heels with tiny spikey studs on them. Maggie hugged Susannah. "Thanks for the invite. Sorry I'm late. That annoying detective paid me a visit again. I'm glad the boys are with their dad this weekend. I'd hate for them to hear all her questions."

"I know. Thank goodness for Bitsy's niece, Andrea. She's a lifesaver." Angie took Maggie's studded purse and stared at it. "She took Caden and Jamal for an afternoon at Chuck E.

Cheese's."

Susannah forced her face to remain placid when she heard Angie's mispronunciation of *Cheese*.

"Oh, you like my costume?" Maggie twirled for Angie, then looked at the table. "All this looks delicious. Sorry I can't stay long, I have a post-Halloween cocktail party with some hairdresser friends this afternoon."

Bitsy moved her chair over. "Come sit by me." She patted the empty seat next to her. All eyes turned to that side of the table as Maggie settled herself, picking up a glass of water and sipping. "Don't keep us waiting, Miss Maggie. Spill."

Maggie put the glass down and surveyed the table. "Right before I was about to leave, I got a knock on my door. Detective Withers, asking more questions about Travis. Only this time she was really harping on whether I ever saw him with drugs." She reached in front of Larraine and plucked a black olive from a glass dish and popped it into her mouth. "Mmmm. Anyway, I told her again, in no uncertain terms, that I would not date someone who took drugs. I have my boys to worry about *and...*" She emphasized the word *and* while reaching for another olive.

Larraine passed her the dish of olives. "And?"

"And I have a business to run, too." She waved at Larraine, as if dismissing the detective. "I've told her that over and over. She just stands there and looks at me with a deadpan face and that frizzy hair." Maggie looked down. "Sorry, I don't mean to be ugly."

Bitsy patted her hand. "I'll let you know when you're being ugly."

Maggie smiled. "Long story short, Travis wasn't just selling stolen guns out of the store, he was dealing drugs." Larraine

CHAPTER THIRTY-EIGHT

gasped, and Bitsy made *tsk, tsk* noises with her tongue. Maggie shook her head and sat back.

"Eat something." Angie served Maggie a slice of lasagna. "You'll feel better."

"The worst part is, Gus Arnold was buying from him." Maggie picked up her fork. "You could have knocked me over with a feather."

"Gus was using drugs?" A melancholy expression crossed Angie's face.

"Uh-huh," Maggie answered, cutting into the lasagna with her fork. "When they interviewed his wife, they found out that his drug use was the reason they separated."

"Gus was married?" Angie's voice pitched higher than usual. "I, I—"

"Divorced," Maggie said, patting Angie's arm. "Sorry, darlin'. Divorced. But she had been in touch with him before he died. He told her he had cleaned up his life."

"I suspected something like this," Susannah said.

"You did?" Keith asked. "What made you think drugs were involved?"

"Well," Susannah said uncomfortably, "I don't usually divulge what's in a patient's health history, but since he's gone now…"

"Spit it out, Suzie," snapped Angie. She heard her strident tone and cringed, then mouthed *sorry*.

"A lot of people knew Gus had a knee injury, but what they didn't know was that he was prescribed opioids by the VA doctor. He had been in pain for years, and it doesn't take long to get addicted."

"Sounds right," Maggie said. "Travis saw a doctor at the VA Medical Center in Atlanta for his injuries, also. He told me they've changed how they work with veterans who have ongoing pain problems. He was pretty angry about it, too. They used to prescribe lots of opioid medication, but now they prescribe other medications and send the veteran to group counseling to deal with the chronic pain."

"But," Tina said, "Gus told me the adjustments helped him get off the pain medications."

"He told me that too," Larraine agreed.

"Well," Maggie said, "I guess by then he was already mixed up with Travis and Owen."

Larraine sat up and looked around. "That's just a shame."

"C'mon. Eat while it's hot," Angie said.

The silence was broken only by murmurs of delight and the occasional clink of flatware. Angie raised her glass for a toast, but before she could speak, there was a knock on the door.

Bitsy rose quickly. "Imma tell whoever it is to go away."

"I got it, you eat." Susannah wiped her hands on her napkin and went to the door. Looking through the peephole, she inhaled sharply. "*Madonna!*"

Outside stood Detective Withers.

CHAPTER THIRTY-NINE

Misalignment and Murder

"Dr. Shine, I'm glad I caught you at home."

Over her shoulder, Susannah saw the detective's car parked between Bitsy's SUV and Larraine's Mercury Grand Marquis. *Great detective work*, Susannah thought. "I've got a house full at the moment."

"That's what I thought. I've got something for Officer Cawthorn. Is he here?"

All eyes were on them as they entered the kitchen.

"Officer Cawthorn." The detective took some papers out of a portfolio and handed them to Keith. "Chief Laughton has authorized me to present you with your official reinstatement. He thought you would be anxious to have it."

Tina clapped and hugged Keith. There were well-wishes from around the table. He smiled. "This is quicker than I hoped."

"Officer Chaffin made a full confession about his theft of weapons from the evidence room and his side business with Travis Keene. He provided the weapons, and they split the profits. He even admitted that he stole your gun." She nodded at Keith. "As insurance. In case he needed to implicate someone else on the force. Though he claims Travis's death was an accident."

"What about Gus?" Angie asked. "Did he confess to that?"

"No. Owen claims Travis killed Gus."

Maggie gasped. "I knew he was a lowdown dog, but I never thought he was a killer."

After swigging her last sip, Bitsy plunked her glass down. "None of us can figure how Gus knew Travis."

"According to Owen, Gus met Travis in Tussahaw Junction. At the time, Gus was looking for OxyContin, and Travis helped him find it."

"I knew Doyle Etheridge was on to something," said Susannah.

The detective turned toward Susannah. "Who?"

"A patient who grew up in the Junction. He thought there were criminals using the woods down that way to hide out."

"Gang crime is an ongoing problem in that area." Detective Withers paused. "But since Travis Keene had never been arrested, we can't connect him with any of that activity. Owen admitted that he knew Travis was selling drugs and Gus had been one of his customers but was no longer using. Owen helped Travis cook up the scheme to keep Gus from talking."

"What scheme?" Angie paled, her Marvelous Magenta standing out as her face turned ashen.

"Owen provided Travis with the guns he sold you and Dr. Shine. Owen cussed up and down about how greedy Travis was to do that. I guess he didn't think the whole situation through. When Owen got wind of the internal investigation, he wanted them back. He demanded that Travis find a way to trade them out with legit guns. Travis asked Gus to help get yours back." The detective pointed at Angie.

CHAPTER THIRTY-NINE

Angie deflated. "Sometimes he seemed more interested in the gun than me."

"Don't feel bad, sweetie." Bitsy patted her hand. "I heard Gus's ex-wife told the police that he had cleaned up his act and was bragging about a new girlfriend." She looked at the detective. "Allegedly."

At this news, Angie perked up.

Detective Withers continued, "Travis thought if he got Gus involved with the stolen guns, there was a better chance Gus wouldn't squeal about Travis's drug business."

"Oh what a tangled web we weave," Larraine said.

"But why did Travis kill Gus?" Susannah asked.

"Owen says they got into an argument when Gus was trading out Angie's gun. That's why Angie's gun was found at the scene. Owen knew the gun was still in Gus's car, and he was trying to sneak it out when one of the other officers found him. He pretended he had just found it on the ground."

"I wish I could jerk a knot in his tail," Keith said, "but it's too late."

Susannah picked at her lasagna. "How does Crystal fit into all this?"

"She has a long history of drug abuse. That's the real reason Travis left her. And according to Owen, she's unstable. He claims she stalked Travis. She knew he was going to be at the scout camp and followed him there. Travis told Owen she was in a bad way, and he took her home. We don't know anything else."

"What was she doing at Maggie's?"

The detective shook her head. "We have her in custody, but we can't interview her. She's not making much sense. She blames Maggie for breaking up her marriage. And she thinks it's your fault, Dr. Shine, that Gus turned on them. Apparently, he was able to wean himself off the drugs because your manipulation of his knee cured his pain."

"And he got murdered for it." Larraine shook her head sadly. "This is just a lot to digest."

"All to make a few bucks." Susannah sat down and put her fists under her chin. "But why was Crystal at Owen's house yesterday?"

"Owen claimed that Crystal was now stalking him and asking him for money to buy drugs. Travis's funeral set her back a pretty penny. When she saw you there, she lost it."

There was silence around the table. The detective took her leave, and as Susannah returned from seeing her to the door, Angie was serving Bitsy another piece of lasagna.

Holding her fork poised for attack, Bitsy said, "I told you Crystal was a few M&M's short of a pack."

Laughter erupted from around the table, and Bitsy held up her fork and smiled.

Susannah looked around the table, happy that her family was together again.

«« » »

If you enjoyed this story, sign up to my Cozy Club Newsletter. Get updates, special content, and news on my next releases. Click here to sign up, and get a FREE e-book from Cathy Tully Cozy Author

If you like what you read, please consider leaving me a review. For Amazon: https://www.amazon.com/dp/B08T8LT69B

Angie's Italian Frittata

Ingredients

- 2 tablespoons olive oil divided
- ½ pound Italian turkey sausage, casings removed
- 1 small onion, chopped
- 1 red or green bell pepper, chopped
- 3-4 small red potatoes, thinly sliced
- 1 teaspoon sea salt
- ½ teaspoon pepper
- 8 large eggs
- 1-2 cloves garlic, sliced thin or pressed
- 2 teaspoons fresh oregano leaves

Instructions

Pre-Heat Oven to 350 Degrees

1. In a large (15-inch) oven-proof skillet, heat 1 tablespoon of the oil. Cook the sausage and potato over medium heat, stirring frequently to keep potato from sticking. Break sausage into 1-inch pieces (or smaller) with your spatula, until browned, about 5 minutes.
2. Add the remaining oil to the skillet. Saute the onion and peppers over medium heat, (scraping up any bits of potato or sausage from the bottom of the pan) until very soft and

caramelized, about 10 minutes.
3. Add garlic and stir.
4. Meanwhile, in a large mixing bowl, beat the eggs with 1/2 teaspoon salt until the yolk and whites are very well combined.
5. Season the mixture with the remaining ½ teaspoon salt and arrange the veggies in an even layer. Reduce the heat to low and pour the eggs over the sausage and vegetables, making sure the pan is evenly coated with eggs. Cook until the sides are set and there's just a shallow layer of uncooked eggs on the top, about 5 minutes.
6. Sprinkle the oregano over the top, if using, and transfer the pan to the broiler. Cook for 2 minutes, until the top is cooked and beginning to lightly brown. Remove from the oven and allow the frittata to sit in the pan for at least 5 minutes before slicing.
7. Cut into wedges and serve alone or on Italian bread.

Larraine's Three Cheese Macaroni and Cheese.

INGREDIENTS

- 1/2 c. (1 stick) butter, plus more for baking dish
- 1 lb. gluten-free pasta (Use any short type, elbow, penne, bowties, shells)
- 1/2 c. gluten-free flour
- 5 c. whole milk
- 1 1/2 tsp. kosher salt
- Freshly ground black pepper
- 3 c. shredded cheddar
- 2 c. shredded Gruyère
- 1 1/2 c. grated Parmesan, divided
- 1 c. gluten-free bread crumbs
- 3 tbsp. extra-virgin olive oil
- Freshly chopped parsley, to garnish

1. Preheat the oven to 350 degrees. Fill a large pot with water and bring to a boil. Add 1 teaspoon salt to the boiling water.
2. Meanwhile, pour milk into a small/medium saucepan and heat over low heat.
3. In another large pot melt 6 tablespoons butter over low

heat. Add the flour and whisk constantly for about 2-3 minutes until smooth.
4. Whisk in hot milk, about 1/2 cup at a time, whisking constantly until sauce slightly thickens. Turn off heat and stir in all the shredded cheese. Add 1/2 teaspoon salt and 1/4 teaspoon pepper.
5. Cook pasta for 1-2 minutes less than the directed time on package, because the noodles will continue to cook in the oven.
6. Drain pasta and combine with the cheese sauce and pour into a baking dish.
7. Melt 2 tablespoons of butter and combine it with the panko. Sprinkle over the macaroni and cheese and bake for 25-30 minutes until cheese is bubbly and the crumbs are lightly golden.

Angie's Pepperoni Lasagna with Marinara sauce

Ingredients
1 (16 ounce) package lasagna noodles
4 cups ricotta cheese
¼ cup grated Parmesan cheese
4 eggs
salt and pepper to taste
1 teaspoon olive oil
3 cloves garlic, minced
1 (32 ounce) jar pasta sauce
1 teaspoon Italian seasoning
1 (16 ounce) block of whole milk mozzarella cheese halved. Dice one half, shred the other.
¼ stick pepperoni cubed

Directions

1. Preheat oven to 350 degrees F (175 degrees C). Bring a large pot of lightly salted water to a boil. Add pasta and cook for 8 to 10 minutes or until al dente; drain and lay lasagna flat on foil to cool.
2. In a medium bowl, combine ricotta, diced mozzarella, pepperoni, Parmesan, eggs, salt and pepper; mix well.

3. In a medium saucepan, heat oil over medium heat and saute garlic for 2 minutes; stir in spaghetti sauce and Italian seasoning. Heat sauce until warmed through, stirring occasionally, 2 to 5 minutes.
4. Spread 1/2 cup of sauce in the bottom of a 9 x13 baking dish. Cover with a layer of noodles. Spread half the ricotta mixture over noodles; top with another noodle layer. Pour 1 1/2 cups of sauce over noodles, and spread the remaining ricotta over the sauce. Top with remaining noodles and sauce and sprinkle mozzarella over all. Cover with greased foil.
5. Bake 45 minutes, or until cheese is bubbly and top is golden.

Glossary

Fall Festival – A fair or festivities centered on harvest/autumn themes. May feature hayrides, pumpkin decorating, scarecrows, and such. Popular at elementary schools in Georgia as fundraisers.

Gavone – Literally gluttonous eater. Used to mean someone who is low class, inappropriately dressed, or rude.

Ghostface – Ghost mask worn in the movie Scream, with an ultra-long open mouth.

Madonna – Used to express shock. Invokes the Virgin Mary, so it better be shocking.

Madonna mia – As above.

Mamalukes – Dumb, idiot.

Mangia – Eat.

Mannaggia – Damn / Cursing.

Puttanna – Loose woman.

Trunk-or-Treat – A variation on Trick-or-Treat where a large parking lot is filled with cars that are decorated for Halloween. Children dressed in costumes go from car to car asking for candy using the phrase 'Trick-or-Treat'. This is in lieu of having children go door to door.

About the Author

Cathy Tully is the pen name of E.C. Tully, a chiropractor and writer. She writes the Dr. Susannah Shine ChiroCozy Mystery Series. She lives in Georgia with her husband and rescue cats.

You can connect with me on:
- https://ectully.com
- https://twitter.com/ChiroCozy
- https://www.facebook.com/CathyTullyCozyAuthor

Subscribe to my newsletter:
- https://bookhip.com/DPRNSB

Also by Cathy Tully

Cathy Tully's Dr. Shine Cracks the Case is Book #1 in the Dr. Susannah Shine ChiroCozy Mystery Series. A light-hearted cozy mystery featuring quirky small-town characters, southern charm, and recipes.

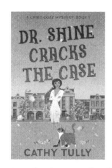

Dr. Shine Cracks the Case
A corpse, a chiropractor, and a cop.

Life in small-town Georgia is the pits. When Dr. Susannah Shine finds the body of a local restaurateur on her doorstep, her cozy life in Peach Grove is flipped upside down. Going full gumshoe, the ex-NYC cop must unearth long-hidden secrets to track down the killer. Along with her peachy BFF, Bitsy, Susannah must hunt down a list of suspects while staying one-step ahead of the detective who's accusing her of a murder she didn't commit.

Made in the USA
Columbia, SC
22 January 2024